# The House at the End of Ferry Road

Beth looked up. A huge shape, like a giant insect, was flying through the sky. She found herself running towards the glasshouse. There was somebody near it. A boy! Beth was shouting but she didn't know what. Her cries broke off as a sudden pain shot through her ankle. She was falling, trees, ground and sky spinning crazily around her. The terrible creature in the sky was almost over her. Four black shapes dropped from its belly. She heard a SPLASH, SPLASH, THUD then BOOM. In the instant before losing consciousness, Beth saw a red s⸻ ⸻. Her body shook ⸻ flew upwards, th⸻

# Hippo Ghost

# The House at the End of Ferry Road

# Martin Oliver

Scholastic Children's Books
7–9 Pratt Street, London NW1 0AE, UK
a division of Scholastic Publications Ltd
London ~ New York ~ Toronto ~ Sydney ~ Auckland

First published by Scholastic Publications Ltd, 1995

Text copyright © Martin Oliver, 1995

ISBN 0 590 13164 8

All rights reserved
Typeset by TW Typesetting, Midsomer Norton, Avon
Printed by Cox & Wyman Ltd, Reading, Berks.

10 9 8 7 6 5 4 3

*To Andrea*

# Chapter 1

"I've got some good news," Gran said. "Mum and Dad have found a new place. You'll be moving in together – in a week's time."

Beth smiled with delight at Gran then glanced across the breakfast table at her brother, Jack. He was sitting with his mouth open in surprise, giving her a full view of his teeth covered in half-chewed cereal and milk.

Jack was two years younger than Beth. He was smaller than his sister and had straight, fair hair like their dad. He was OK as kid brothers go, Beth thought, but there were two things about him that were really annoying.

The worst thing was that he always looked neat and tidy. Even if he played football at school at lunchtime, he would never come home with grass stains on his clothes or dirt clinging to his shoes. Even if everyone else in his team looked like abominable mud monsters, Jack would appear clean, well-scrubbed and without a hair out of place.

This wouldn't have mattered so much to Beth if she hadn't always looked the exact opposite. As someone had once said, she didn't look as if she'd been dragged through a hedge backwards – she looked more as though she'd just been on a roller-coaster ride through a food-throwing machine.

It was almost magical – she only had to walk into a kitchen for a dollop of tomato sauce to appear from nowhere and drip on to her white school shirt. If it hadn't rained for weeks you could guarantee that Beth would find the one tiny puddle that hadn't dried up and that her best summer gear would get smeared with soggy black yuk.

It wasn't even as if she tried to look scruffy.

In the morning, Beth would do her shoelaces up, tuck in her shirt and pull back her hair like everyone else. It wasn't her fault that, for some reason, during the day her laces would wriggle out of their knots, her shirt would come untucked, and her black, curly hair would escape from its confines and blow around in the breeze.

Beth was always getting comments on how scruffy she looked and she always got blamed for any mess left around the house. All adults would do was take a look at this scruffy girl towering over her neat brother and suspect that she was the culprit of any mischief – it just wasn't fair.

Still, what Beth lacked in neatness she made up for in quick wits. She had suspected something was going to be announced when she caught the extra edge of urgency in Gran's voice telling them to hurry up and come downstairs. Then, when they had all started eating breakfast and Gran had switched off the TV, Beth definitely knew something important would be said.

But the announcement had caught Jack by surprise. Beth looked at him. His mouth was opened wide in mid-munch. Surely he was going to spill milk on to his clothes. Just this once it would happen. A tiny fraction of a second more and the milk would dribble on to … Jack's jaw snapped shut. Beth sighed. It would have been too good to be true. She shifted her gaze across to their gran.

"So where are we going to live?" she asked. "They've found somewhere near where your dad works. It's all going very quickly and should be sorted out in a few days. Then you can all move in together."

Beth and Jack grinned at each other. This was good news. Their dad had found a new job in London just before the summer term had ended. He had come home and told them that he had been head-hunted. That had worried Jack until Beth explained what the word meant nowadays. They had sold their old home quickly but couldn't find anywhere new. As a result, Mum had decided that Jack and Beth should move in with their gran when school ended, while she and Dad looked in earnest.

"Do you know what it's like?" Jack asked. "If it's near London it might be close to Heathrow or Gatwick."

Beth groaned. Jack's other annoying habit was his crazes. They rarely lasted longer than a few months but while he was in the grip of them, he would talk or think of very little else. At the moment he was into planes. He had lots of books showing little pictures of all the planes that had ever been built. The pages were full of pictures and boring information about planes. Jack had bought model plane kits which he had made and pinned up above his bed. He would be glued to the television if any films about flying were on and he had picked up the jargon pilots used.

"I hope not, Biggles," Beth replied. "I don't want great, noisy, smelly planes ruining my beauty sleep."

"You certainly need a lot of that," Jack replied. Beth decided to say nothing. Instead she stuck her tongue out at him.

"That's enough, you two," Gran said. "Actually your mum and dad were a bit vague about the details. They're certain you'll like the house but I think they want it to be a bit of a surprise."

"I bet it's a haunted house," Jack said in a spooky voice. "It was cursed by a previous owner and is in the middle of a graveyard. At midnight, zombies come up out of the ground and chase anyone who's there." Zombies had been another of Jack's crazes.

"And they'll be covered in zombie ooze," Beth continued. "And if their sinister slime touches you it will turn you into one of them." She flicked a spoonful of marmalade at Jack. A tiny dollop actually hit him. Beth ignored the rest that had dropped on to her lap and continued, "Oh no, he's already becoming a zombie – look at his eyes, his hands, his face – they're horrible!"

"Ha, ha, very funny. Actually, that's not how you get turned into a zombie at all."

"All right, you two," Gran interrupted. "Break it up now. I take it that means breakfast is finished. I'll do the washing up today. I don't trust you to do it, not after last night; I value my crockery too much. Do you think you could keep yourselves out of mischief for the next few minutes?"

They both stood up, grinning, delighted to have got away with not doing the chores. While Jack dashed out of the room, Beth suddenly remembered the marmalade she had dropped on to her lap. She was too late to stop it sludging down her jeans and landing on the kitchen floor. "Oh, no," she muttered to herself. Before Gran noticed the mess, she quickly scraped it up then slipped upstairs to find a wet cloth.

Back in her room, her attempts to clean off the marmalade only seemed to make matters worse. She was considering whether to change when Jack burst through the door. His arms were held out at either side and he was making a noise that was supposed to sound like a plane's engine. "Mayday, mayday! This is golf, foxtrot, tango. Our position is unknown, we have got one engine on fire and are running out of fuel… Oh, no, engine number three has gone… Mayday, mayday, I can't hold her, we're going to have to crash land the old crate in the drink. Brace yourselves…"

With that, he circled twice around Beth's bed then dived on to it. After a few seconds, he looked through the pillows and duvet at his sister. Beth was staring at him with an unamused expression on her face.

"You're a right pain, you are. Next time you want to barge in here with your silly games, will you knock?"

"OK, OK, keep your hair on," Jack said. "I only wanted to talk about the new house."

Beth sighed. Jack was always interrupting her when she wanted to do something on her own, but she remembered that her mum had told her to look after him while they were away. She was the oldest so it was up to her to take care of him and besides, if she ignored him he might be even more of a nuisance.

"What do you think it will be like?" Jack asked. "Seriously, now. Gran must know a bit more than she said."

Beth shrugged. "I hope it's a big old house with a big garden. Maybe a walled garden with tangled, overgrown bushes and secret clearings."

"I don't think Dad would be too keen on that," Jack replied. "You know what he's like with gardening. You might be right about an old house, though. I want the attic room if it's got one. It would be great for watching planes and as a lookout post."

"An attic *would* be good," Beth agreed, eyes lighting up at the thought. "It might be full of old relics. Maybe it was owned by an explorer who left a trunk full of souvenirs. We might find some old clothes or photo albums. Or it could have been the home of a mad inventor who left books and—"

"Come off it, sis," Jack snorted. Beth was always going off making up ridiculous stories and imagining things. It was so embarrassing. On holiday in Scotland, there had been Beth's Loch Ness Monster that turned out to be a log in the water. Then there was the next door neighbour who Beth had accused of being a grave robber but who turned out to be a road digger who worked nights. And of course there had been the yeti-sighting at his birthday party, not to mention the infamous "burglar" episode. Why had he been lumbered with a sister with a hyperactive imagination?

Jack's thoughts were broken by the doorbell ringing. He and Beth heard Gran's welcome, then footsteps tramped up the stairs. They watched as the door swung open and a familiar face appeared around it. With her long brown hair tied back and green eyes sparkling, it was Mum!

"Hello, you two," she said. "So you've heard the news. We've found somewhere — we're going to be living in a house at the end of Ferry Road."

# Chapter 2

"Are we there yet?" Jack asked.

"Just a bit longer now. We'll be there soon, don't worry."

Beth squinted out of the open window at the unfamiliar surroundings. It was a very warm day and by now the air inside the car felt stale and uncomfortable.

The last week had passed by in a whirl. Beth and Jack had been both nervous and excited and could think of little else apart from the move. Although staying with their gran was fun, they couldn't wait to find out about their new home. They had bombarded Mum with so many questions that she had covered her ears with her hands. Once they had quietened down she had reached into her bag and pulled out a sheet of paper from the estate agent's.

Jack and Beth's eyes had swallowed up the information on the paper. A small, blurred black and white photograph showed them an ordinary looking house. Underneath it were the typed details which described number 35 Ferry Road as a brand new "desirable residence".

Beth's heart sank. There went all her hopes of finding interesting bits and pieces left by former owners. She carried on reading. The piece of paper told her that the property enjoyed a lounge/dining room, three bed-rooms and a gge.

"What's a gge?" Jack asked.

"It's short for garage," Mum replied. "Any more questions before I get on?"

"It's not built on a graveyard is it, by any chance?"

Mum shook her head in bewilderment at Jack's question. "No, it isn't, but we think

12

you'll both really like it. I'll leave this with you for now. I've got lots of things to do."

With that, Mum had settled down by the phone and begun dialling. Beth and Jack looked at each other. Disappointment mingled with eagerness to see their new house.

"I can't see why they think we'll like it. It doesn't look very exciting," Beth said. "Still, at least we can have our own rooms. I wonder which ones we'll get."

The discussion about bedrooms had continued throughout the week until the subject was banned. At last the questions were replaced by pent-up excitement as they set off for their new house. In order to keep them occupied during the journey, Mum had suggested they play Legs and I-spy, both of which Beth had won, to Jack's annoyance. Conversation and interest had died down as they reached the motorway, but now they had turned off and were heading down a long main road flanked by rows of houses.

Beth wound the window down to let the cool draught blow on her face. Shops, a school and some playing fields passed by. On the right Beth noticed signs to a sailing club. At a traffic-light junction Mum pressed the indicator arm and they turned into a tree-lined street.

"We're very nearly there now," said Mum. They drove round a sharp bend then stopped at a roundabout. "This is it," she continued as they turned right. "This is Ferry Road."

Mum drove slowly down the quiet, narrow street. Jack nudged Beth excitedly. Beth noticed a pub, a few shops and some small cottages before they pulled up at the end of the road.

"And this is our new home."

Beth and Jack looked over to where Mum was pointing and their eyes opened wide in astonishment.

"It's on an island," Jack gasped. "Wow."

The car had stopped where the road ended at the river's edge. In front of them was a narrow bridge with signs saying: "Temporary bridge, no heavy loads". The bridge crossed a few metres of shallow, slow-moving brown water and linked Ferry Road with a small island in the river. On the island, Beth and Jack could see three new houses and, jogging out of one of them, Dad!

Beth couldn't quite believe her eyes. She dropped her bag and dashed over the bridge with Jack hot on her heels.

They met Dad halfway across. "Oof! Hello there." He picked Beth up. "How are you then? I've missed you. So what do you think of your old folks then? Did we surprise you?"

"You bet," grinned Beth. "This is brilliant. Is it for real? Are we really going to live on an island? I can't believe it."

"You'd better believe it, kid," Dad replied in his best Humphrey Bogart voice. "We thought you'd like it here."

"It's amazing. You could have told us sooner, though. I never thought we'd be moving on to an island."

"We thought you might get too excited if we told you beforehand. Mind you, it's not really an island. It used to be one but that was before they built the bridge. Once they've strengthened it, we'll be part of Ferry Road."

"I don't care," replied Beth. "It's like being on an island."

"Yes, it is. Come on. Let's explore."

Mum's cries of "Don't run, slow down," were ignored as Beth and Jack raced neck and neck over the bridge and jumped on to the island.

"I claim this land for the Baker family," Beth said, picking up a stick and planting it in the ground. "That's what they used to do in history," she added for Jack's benefit.

But her brother wasn't listening. He had dashed over to the other houses that were on the island. Only number 35 had been completed and the others were in various stages of construction. Jack gazed in fascination at the wooden frame of a roof that looked like the rib cage of a strange creature. Pieces of equipment were dotted around the site, covered in dust and mud. Jack dodged around a cement mixer and began poking at a pile of bricks.

Beth hoped he was out of sight of Mum and Dad. She could almost hear them telling her to keep an eye on her brother.

"This is even better than zombies. I hope no one else buys the houses," Jack said. "Then we'll be like castaways on a desert island – just the four of us."

Beth crossed her eyes at the thought of sharing a desert island with her brother.

"We'll be marooned and we'll have to make a boat to sail away to safety. That's what people do on desert islands."

"And if no one sees us we'll have to eat the smallest member of the family so we don't starve." Beth made her eyes go wide and licked her lips as she stared at Jack. She put her arms out and began to lumber towards him.

"Now then, you two." Dad's voice stopped her. He and Mum were standing in front of number 35. "Come on, you haven't even seen your new home yet."

They set off at a gallop. "Mind that puddle," Jack warned. Beth swerved just in time and smiled – that was a good start. A few steps later they were rattling the front door, eager to look inside.

"Oh, dear, where have I put the key?" Dad asked. "Oh, no, I've lost it!"

Beth noticed the twinkle in his eye as he spoke and reached into his jacket pocket. "OK, OK," he chuckled. "Here it is."

He opened the door and they went inside, where the second surprise of the day was waiting for them. The first batch of furniture had already been delivered and the downstairs was almost completely furnished. "First things first, let's show you around," Mum said.

Beth and Jack nodded and followed their parents around the ground floor. The kitchen didn't really interest them, nor did the downstairs cloakroom or dining room, but Jack did throw himself on to the sofa and declare himself at home. It was funny, Beth thought, seeing their old chairs and sofa in the new surrounding, but they seemed to fit.

The downstairs was bright and sunny but would it pass the most important test? Beth took a deep breath and sucked in the air. It smelt like home already – that musty scent that came from their battered furniture had swirled through the rooms and added a layer of comfortable familiarity. Beth smiled at her mum, who grinned back at her with relief.

"Now for the upstairs," she said, taking a deep breath. "I think you should decide on your rooms once you've seen them."

Mum opened the door to the back bedroom. Beth stepped inside and immediately knew that this should be hers. Somehow everything felt right. It was a light, warm room with a bed in one corner and a bedside table. Her lamp and alarm clock were already on the table as if Mum and Dad had known she would want this room. She glanced out of the window and saw wide open spaces. There was a dense patch of green where the island met the river. Beyond that the river curved away gently towards the blue, cloudless sky.

Beth caught her breath. There was something familiar about that view. She felt as though she had seen it before – only slightly different. No, that was stupid, of course she couldn't have seen it before. She shook her head to clear out the thought. Her mum, misunderstanding Beth's action, looked worried. "Oh, dear..." she began.

"Oh, no," Beth interrupted. "No, I like it – I really do. It's wonderful, I can't wait to get everything unpacked."

Before she could do that however, the tour continued into her parents' room and then up into the attic. Eyes gleaming with excitement, Jack waved Beth up and showed her around the room as if he already owned the place.

"So, does that mean that you're happy with your rooms?" asked Mum. Beth and Jack both nodded. "Good. Well, I'm glad that's settled. Now the fun begins – it's unpacking time."

*Bang, bang, bump!* For the next few hours, the house reverberated to the sounds of wardrobes, chests of drawers, packing cases and other bits and pieces being carried upstairs.

*Rip, tear, attischoo!* The boxes were opened and their dusty contents were tipped out and put away. The rest of the day passed by in a whirl of unpacking, organizing, arranging and tea drinking.

Beth sat on the floor of her bedroom with her possessions in piles of boxes around her and set about making the room hers. Packing everything up from their old house had been a long and sad job. She had been miserable at the thought of leaving their old home and her friends but now they were in their house on Ferry Road her mood was different. Wandering about the house, she already felt at home, even if the taps were the wrong way round so she kept getting cold water instead of hot.

Unpacking proved to be a doddle as well. It was so easy that if Beth closed her eyes and let her imagination drift she could almost see the furniture shuffle into position on unseen feet. Her clothes seemed to fly out of the suitcases, snuggling up in the comforting familiarity of drawers and shelves.

The shout of "Tea's up!" brought Beth out of her dreams. She stood up to admire her work. The room was sparklingly clean and — amazingly — it even looked tidy. Beth knew it would never last, but at least it was a good start.

She wiped her brow. Suddenly she realized how hot and dusty she felt. Her throat was beginning to prickle and her eyes were itching. "I need some fresh air," she thought.

As Beth opened the window, a flash of light caught her gaze. It came from a dense copse of trees and bushes at the edge of the island. While she was looking, a breeze blew along the river, brushing aside the tops of the trees like a hand pulling open a green curtain, allowing her to glimpse what lay behind.

Beth could just make out the remains of a building through the trees. Branches were sticking out of what was once a roof and a crow was standing on what must have been a door-frame. The sun was reflecting off a broken pane of glass. She suddenly realized what the building was – an old glasshouse. She had seen them in books; they were pretty, ornate buildings where people used to grow tropical plants.

Once it must have looked lovely. Beth could picture the plants waving inside their warm sunny house, but now it looked dark and dangerous. The plants had shrivelled away to dust, the iron frame was twisted painfully and shattered glass lay in wait, sharp as daggers, for the unwary visitor.

In the cool draught Beth's red eyes began to fill with tears. As everything became watery and blurred, she noticed something moving. Two figures, children maybe, were running around the glasshouse. For a fleeting second she thought the building had changed too; it looked brand new, just as she had pictured it. Beth blinked several times. The scene dissolved and when she looked again, the figures had gone and the glasshouse was as ruined as ever. Of course she must have been mistaken, she hadn't been seeing clearly.

At that moment, a dark cloud moved in front of the sun, casting a shadow over the scene, and a gust of wind blew down the river. The trees closed in around the glasshouse and the window slammed shut. Beth started as the glass vibrated in its frame. She heard footsteps run up the stairs.

"Are you OK?" Mum asked. "We'll get that

latch fixed tomorrow. Come on down now. Your father's made some tea and I think we ought to try and eat it to please him."

Beth allowed herself to be led out of the door. Before she left the room she glanced back over her shoulder. There was no sign of the glasshouse or the figures behind the thick trees.

"That's one place to explore," Beth said to herself. But for some reason, she didn't feel excited about the thought. She looked out to where the trees hid the ruin and she felt a shiver run down her spine.

# Chapter 3

That night Beth slept a deep and dreamless sleep. She woke up to the sound of curtains being drawn and her mum's voice saying, "Come on, lazybones, breakfast's ready."

Beth groaned and hid her head under the covers until the smell of toast and coffee proved too much for her rumbling stomach. She flung some clothes over her aching limbs and went downstairs. The others were sitting on packing cases around the table. Jack was pouring milk over his cereal and talking excitedly about a Jumbo Jet he had seen earlier from his room.

"So Sleeping Beauty's awake at last," Dad said, grinning. "Hope you slept well on your first night?"

Beth nodded. She buttered her toast and ate it quickly. She was really looking forward to their first full day – there was so much to get excited about. A few minutes later breakfast was over and everything was cleared away into the sink.

"We need to get a few basics. Why don't we explore the shops on Ferry Road?" Dad asked.

"I don't suppose this new interest in shopping has got anything to do with the fact that the washing up needs doing?" Mum replied. "You're staying here. Beth and Jack can get what we want, can't you?"

They were eager to go but waited obediently as Mum scribbled a list on a scrap of paper and gave them some money. Coins jingling in her pockets, Beth rushed out of the door, closely followed by Jack. On the bridge, they turned to wave at their dad, who was staring glumly into the sink.

It was a warm morning and the river sparkled in the sunlight. Everything looked lovely and Beth's spirits were cheered by the thought that they had the whole summer to settle in and explore their new surroundings.

She slowed down as she stepped off the bridge on to Ferry Road. She had only seen it from the car, now she wanted a good look. Beth strolled past some small cottages towards a run of shops. Signs jutting out from walls told her that there was a greengrocer's, a baker's and a newsagent's up ahead. At the far end of the road she spotted a pub called the Ferry Tavern and a red pillar box sheltering under a large, ancient-looking tree.

Jack's footsteps clattering ahead were the only sound that broke the silence that lay like a heavy blanket over the road. The river soaked up any noise from the opposite bank and the traffic from the main road was muffled by intervening streets and trees.

It really is cut off, Beth thought. Almost like a hidden street, a secret place where… Where what might go on? Beth shook her head. She was letting her imagination run away with itself, as usual. Of course everything was normal. It was just a quiet, old-fashioned street. There was Jack running along past the houses towards the shops, oblivious to her thoughts. As she hurried along to catch him up, Beth glanced at the houses on either side. They were small, well-kept cottages with neat gardens at the front and clean net curtains at the windows. Beth noticed there were no satellite dishes anywhere. "It's probably some sort of protected area," she thought.

A snatch of music came floating through the air from one of the houses or maybe one of the shops. It was an old song but it was catchy. Almost without realizing it, Beth picked up the tune and began humming along. Up ahead she saw Jack going into the newsagent's. Beth put her head down and lengthened her stride to catch up with him, half expecting to see a friendly bobby on a bike cycle past.

Instead, she got a shock when she almost collided with a figure who seemed to have come from nowhere and appeared right in front of her. Beth started and stepped back in amazement. A scruffily-dressed man with untidy grey hair was standing in front of her. Anger was imprinted on his face, but when he saw Beth's face his expression changed. His eyes opened wide and he went pale – he looked almost scared.

"Oh, er, I'm sorry," Beth gasped in surprise. "I didn't see you there. I didn't mean to startle you."

The old man recovered quickly. "Out of my way," he muttered angrily, brushing past her.

Beth stared at the retreating figure in amazement, her heart pounding. What a rude old misery guts, she thought. He'd given her a real shock – it certainly wasn't the way she'd imagined the day would start. She hoped everyone else wasn't going to be like him.

She needn't have worried. As soon as she went into the newsagent's, she felt relaxed. In contrast to the exterior it was bright and modern-looking inside. In front of the door was a counter stocked with newspapers and chocolates. Shelves were stacked with magazines and a large fridge was humming in a corner. Jack was already talking to the shop-keeper when Beth walked in. She was about their mum's age with greying hair and a friendly voice.

"Hello," she smiled. "So you must be this young man's sister." Beth nodded while the shopkeeper continued. "It's so nice to see new customers. We don't often get people dropping in except for the regulars."

"Oh," replied Beth, going to the fridge for some milk. "Well, we'll be regulars soon. We've moved into the new house at the end of the road."

Beth noticed that the woman looked at them with added interest. "That's nice. I'm sure you'll like it here, everyone's very friendly."

Beth thought about mentioning the old man but she bit her lip. She wasn't going to let him ruin her first morning. He probably didn't live nearby. She would never see him again so she wasn't going to let him upset her.

"We're hoping some other childen will move in and be our neighbours," Jack replied.

"But we'll be busy until they do. It's our first proper day here today. We've got lots of places to explore and I've got lots of planes to spot."

Beth decided to rescue the shopkeeper before she was interrogated about her knowledge of aeroplanes. "We need some sugar, do you have any?"

"It's just been delivered, but I haven't put it on the shelves yet."

The newsagent disappeared into the back of the shop. By the time she came back with a packet in her hand, Beth and Jack had found the other things on their list. They paid for the shopping and as they turned to leave, the newsagent smiled and wished them a happy time in Ferry Road.

"She was nice," Jack said as the shop's door shut behind them. "Now, have we got everything? Can we head back?"

Beth shook her head and pointed left along the road. She opened her mouth to tell him where they had to go next but her words were drowned out by a loud shout.

"Come along, ladies and gentlemen. Get

your fruit and veg here. Lov-er-ly, ripe fruit. Get your strawberries 'ere, all your strawbs."

A short distance along the street was the greengrocer's. Jack and Beth stared at the man who was standing, arms crossed, in front of his shop. He was short and bandy-legged, and his head was topped with a mass of thick orange hair. He had just finished arranging a colourful display of fruit and vegetables which were shaded by a stripy awning. He looked around, then suddenly changed his voice to imitate that of an old lady and began a loud, imaginary conversation, changing his voice with every other sentence.

"Ooh, they look nice."

"They're lovely, they are…"

"…and very good value too."

"Lov-er-ly, jubbly. There we are, madam…"

He broke off as he spotted the two children staring up at him. "Now, what can I do for you two? How about some fruit? Makes your hair curly…" He broke off when he saw Beth's hair but the pause was only momentary. He looked at Jack. "Puts hair on your chest…"

Jack's expression made him falter once again but he carried on bravely, "Come along now ladies and gents, how about two punnets for £1.50, three for £2.25? I can't say fairer than that, can I?"

"Really, Mr W. Stop giving these children a hard time. They won't swallow that ridiculous sales patter of yours. Don't you worry about him, he's always like this."

Beth and Jack looked further down the road to find out who had just spoken. They saw a tall man standing in the doorway of the bakery. He gave them a reassuring nod. When they looked back, the greengrocer beamed down at them, showing off a gold filling in his front tooth.

"I'm only drumming up a bit of business. Anyway, you know that Honest Reg White wouldn't play tricks on anyone." He pointed proudly to the sign above his shop. "White's the greengrocer's, family business since 1873. We've been here for generations and service is our middle name. Actually, Vernon's my middle name. That's my son's name too. You may have heard of him, Vernon White, estate agent?"

Jack shook his head. Mr White sighed, then whispered loudly to them. "You're new around here, aren't you? Well, take my advice and take no notice of old Bob the baker. He's a worrier, like his family before him."

The baker piped up again. "Now then, don't you listen to him and don't let him make you buy anything you don't really want. He comes from a long line of rogues — good-natured rogues, but rogues nonetheless. And don't you try to deny it, we all know about your dad…"

Beth detected a hint of pride in the green-grocer's voice. "Even during the war, he could always produce a banana for a special treat…"

"…and at a special price too, so my mother told me," the baker added.

"We'd like some apples, please," said Beth.

Mr White turned to the two children. "Of course. I've got a special offer for you, two pounds for a pound."

"And how much for one pound?"

"Fifty pence."

"Not much of a special offer, is it?" Beth said.

She heard the baker laugh on the other side of the street. "I thought she'd be too sharp to fall for your old tricks," he grinned.

"All right then," the greengrocer said. "Here are your apples and here's one extra each. Go on now, or you'll be bad for business." His voice was stern but Beth and Jack noticed a twinkle in his eye as he spoke.

They carried on down the street munching their apples and stopped outside the bakery. The baker had gone inside his shop and they could see him sweeping and tidying up. A delicious smell was wafting out of the shop. The window contained a mouth-watering assortment of bread, cakes and other goodies but, unlike the untidy mass of colours at Mr White's, the baker had arranged his food with almost military precision.

Jack suggested that they needed a dough-nut for elevenses and Beth eagerly agreed. The baker politely introduced himself as Mr Stevens.

"I hope you didn't feel it was improper of

me to intrude upon your conversation with Mr White," he said, tugging at the ends of his neatly trimmed moustache. "We've known each other for years," he added. "Our fathers used to own these shops and their fathers before them. Now, how can I help?"

Beth and Jack chose some bread and goodies for everyone. As they left, the baker held the door open for them and they strolled back down Ferry Road towards the bridge.

"That's it," Beth said. "So what do you think?"

"It's OK. Mr White was funny and I can't wait to try all the cakes in the bakery," came Jack's reply. "But I'm hungry now. We should eat our doughnuts and dump the shopping before we do some more exploring. Beth! Come on, Beth!"

Beth grunted. Her attention had been caught by an interesting-looking shop, set back from the road between the cottages and the shops. In contrast to the rest of the street it was run-down and battered about the edges. The front of the shop was covered in a wild-looking green plant with dark purple flowers. The shoots of the plant swayed in the breeze, moving like fingers, eager to find new walls to cling to. Paint was flaking off the shop's door and the window panes were dusty and cracked. Several interesting-looking objects – an old gramophone, a desk – could be made out behind the layer of grime. One thing in particular stood out. Slightly apart from the other items was a chunky, arch-shaped wooden box. It was intriguing. Beth wanted to know what it was.

"Oh, come on. Let's go home. I'm starving!"

Beth stood for a moment before nodding reluctantly. While her brain wanted her to investigate the shop, the thought of elevenses was making her stomach agree with Jack. Oh, well, I'll come for another look when Jack isn't around, she decided, before saying, "OK, then. Home it is."

# Chapter 4

Over the next few days the Bakers gradually unpacked all their things, emptied out the cardboard boxes, packed some cases away and began to settle properly into their new home. After less than a week it was already difficult to believe that they hadn't always been there. The sun had shone every day and the newness of eating makeshift meals out of doors reminded Beth of their camping holidays.

But there was never so much work to do on their holidays. Even after unpacking, hundreds more jobs seemed to crop up. Indoors, furniture was repositioned and rooms rearranged while outside, the garden only began to take shape after many hours of digging and planting.

Despite being so busy, Beth found herself spending a lot of time thinking about the junk shop on Ferry Road and especially the curious box she had noticed. It was strange but she just couldn't get it out of her mind. She really wanted to know what it was. She had mentioned it to Jack but once he knew it was old but almost certainly wasn't a pirate treasure chest, he lost interest. On a couple of occasions she had been driven past the shop but there had been no time to stop and go inside. She had also tried to sneak off during the day to get a closer look only to be stopped by a call from Mum or Dad, wanting her to do something around the house.

During the evenings, she and Jack wandered around the half-finished houses, while in the daytime they took quick breathers to watch the workmen who were constantly disappearing into the houses then reappearing at various doors and windows. Beth thought that she had better stop complaining about moving furniture when she saw what the builders were shifting.

The workmen were friendly and Beth and Jack used to go over to give them extra supplies for their lunch and tea breaks. They were told about the crane that had lifted heavy equipment on to the island, enabling the houses to be built, but their favourite stories were the tales of finding coins under floorboards and diaries bricked up inside chimneys.

"I wish these were old houses. Then you might have found something interesting here," Beth had said.

In reply, the foreman had smiled enigmatically and told them to keep an eye open. "You never know when you might find something from the past," he said. "Sometimes things appear when you're least expecting them."

The offers of lifts in wheelbarrows and a chance to go upstairs in the unfinished houses were eagerly accepted, although Beth regretted it later when Mum wanted to know how her clothes had got into such a mess. However, she was quickly forgiven when her new-found friends were able to help. Connor, the site chippy, put his carpentry skills to good use when he rescued some of Dad's DIY, or Disaster-It-Yourself as it was usually called.

His workmate, Brian the sparky, had been even more helpful a couple of nights later. It had all been a bit spooky really. The sun had begun dipping under the horizon and the builders were still on site, working late to finish the other houses. Dad was in the lounge watching TV while Mum was sitting by the table playing through some tapes to find the track she wanted. Beth had been feeling peckish. She went into the kitchen to fix herself a snack.

"Would you turn the kettle on while you're there?" Mum had asked.

Beth had crossed to the far wall, passing the front window as she did. The blind was drawn. Although she couldn't see the work-men, she could hear them packing up their things. She reached over and hit the switch.

*Ffffzzzz, bang!* Suddenly the lights went

out, the television died and the tape player ground to a halt.

"What the…? What's going on?"

"I don't know."

"It must be a fuse," came a loud groan. "I'll fix it." The sound of Dad getting out of his chair was closely followed by a crash and muffled curses.

"It's OK. I'm nearest. I'll do it," Beth said, addressing the pitch darkness. The change from light to dark had been so sudden that her eyes hadn't had a chance to get used to it. She could have been talking to an empty house for all she could see. A sudden stupid fear overtook her for a second. "Are you there?" she called. Mum's calm answer, that she would lend a hand as soon as she'd got Dad safely sitting down out of the way, quickly reassured her.

Beth left the kitchen and stepped out into the corridor. She peered into the gloom, gradually making out different textures and patterns in the blank blackness. What was that shadow? Was someone moving? No, her mind was playing tricks on her. It was only a curtain flapping in the breeze.

Beth continued slowly, trying to feel her way along the wall. "Ow!" She banged her toe on a chair. Someone must have moved it during the day – this was worse than an obstacle course, she thought. She took another step. That was fine. Another step and another, and she was nearly at the fuse box. She was just about to open it when...

"Yeeoooow!" A huge insect landed on her shoulder, hairy, tickly legs crawling over her bare flesh. Beth squirmed and flapped away at it in a panic.

The insect disappeared. Beth stood still for a moment, waiting for her heart to stop pounding. At that moment she saw a light appear a few paces away from her. It was shining upwards, casting a red light on a hideous face that seemed to float above the ground. It was a ghost!

"Oooooh," wavered the ghost.

"Help!" yelled Beth.

"Oooooh ... ooh ... ha, ha..." The ghost

collapsed into a fit of giggles. "Got you," it said. "That fooled you – you should have seen your face."

"Jack!" Beth shouted. "Just you wait. I'll get you. Stop it, you little—" She put her arms up as Jack shone the torch straight into her eyes.

"All right. Pack it in. Jack, if you want to shine the torch, will you shine it so I can change this fuse?" Mum patted Beth on her shoulder as she moved past. Jack hid on the other side of her legs as Beth tried to get her hands on him.

"Pack it in, I said," Mum repeated. "Can you hold the torch still for a minute?"

Beth's protests fell on deaf ears. Mum slotted in the new fuse. She hit the switch and the lights came back on. Beth stared at her brother. She was determined to get her own back, although she would have to wait for the right moment for revenge. Luckily the chance came more quickly than she had expected. No sooner had everything started up in the kitchen than the fuse blew again.

"It must be a fault in the wiring. We need an electrician."

Beth gave Jack a hefty shove and was pleased to hear him fly backwards down the corridor. "I've seen Brian working on the other houses today," she piped up. "He's a sparky. If we hurry outside, we may catch him."

They found Brian and he managed to fix the wiring. Her parents were so pleased that they even ignored Jack's complaints about his bruised elbow and told him that he had got what he deserved. Although that cheered Beth up, she still didn't forgive her brother. The following day they ignored each other and went about on their own. They helped their parents in the morning then they were given the afternoon off – "for good behaviour", Mum joked.

While Jack stayed on the island, Beth decided to head for Ferry Road. Now she had a chance to visit the shop without dragging Jack around after her. From the bridge, she noticed that Ferry Road was much busier than the first time she had been there. A stream of cars and shoppers was flowing along the road and Beth could hear the greengrocer going through his theatrical selling routine.

She saw the baker locking up his shop before walking into one of the cottages further down the road. A minute or so later, he reappeared with three dogs. Beth watched their owner untangle himself from their leads. She giggled as the dogs, who the baker called Wellington, Nelson and Monty, totally ignored the baker's brisk commands and pulled him along behind them.

She stepped off the bridge but her smile faded after she had wandered up and down the road for a few minutes. Even though she thought she knew where it was, it took longer than she had expected to find the junk shop. Somehow she had managed to walk past it.

"This place really is tucked away. No wonder it's not doing too well," thought Beth, beginning to feel a bit hot and bothered. She turned the doorhandle and pushed. The door didn't move. Beth pulled. The response was the same.

"Don't say it's closed," muttered Beth. She moved away from the door. Using her hand to shield her eyes from the sunlight, she peered in through the glass panes. There was the desk and the gramophone and there was the tall arch-shaped wooden box that had been on her mind. What was it? Craning her neck, Beth saw some buttons sticking out on the front of the box but that was all. She tutted crossly. This was annoying. She still couldn't work out what it was.

Beth's gaze moved away from the object to the rest of the shop. The sunlight did not penetrate the gloom beyond the window. She squinted hard, moving her head from side to side but she could see nothing. She was about to turn away when something moved. There, half in the shadow, half in the light, Beth thought she saw a girl. And was that a boy behind her?

She moved her head slightly but all she saw was her own face in the glass. Of course, that was it. There was nobody in the shop, she had just seen her reflection. Beth pulled a face at herself, then she caught sight of someone behind her. Half-hidden behind a car was someone who seemed to be staring at her. With a jolt, Beth recognized him. It was the old man who had been so rude to her.

Beth whirled around. The bright sunlight blinded her temporarily and by the time she could see clearly again, the man was just visible walking away further up the road. Beth rubbed her eyes. Who was the man? Had he been watching her?

No, don't be so stupid, she told herself. He was probably just walking past and saw me looking into the shop. If I hadn't seen his reflection in the glass, I'd never even have noticed him. Of course he isn't watching me.

Beth felt cross with herself. As usual, she'd got herself worked up over nothing. She was aware that her heart was pounding and that made her feel more irritable. She set off briskly for home, feeling uncomfortable in the hot sun. She found herself walking on auto-pilot; her legs seemed to know the way back and she let them take her home. I'd better wait for the boat, she found herself thinking.

Beth shook her head. What boat? She opened her eyes and looked around in astonishment. She was standing by the water's edge, several metres away from the bridge. What was she thinking of?

"It must be the heat scrambling my brains," she decided. "A drink is all I need to get a grip on things."

A glass of ice-cold squash did refresh her but she was quiet for the rest of the day. In the evening, she hardly listened to Jack's account of finding an old brick wall behind some bushes as she concentrated on putting the incident at the shop and her daydream out of her mind.

A good night's sleep really did the trick and the next day Beth woke up feeling rested and refreshed. She even forgave her brother for the ghost trick and they began talking to each other again. After lunch they watched from various vantage points as other families and couples came to see the houses and then tried to guess which of them were responsible for the SOLD stickers that appeared at the front windows of the houses.

Jack's curiosity about the house buyers wrestled with his wish for them to have the island to themselves. "I hope that lot with the three girls don't move in, or the wrinklies," he muttered.

That had earned him a sharp reprimand. Beth kept quiet. She would like some people her age to play with but they would have to wait and see. Nobody would move in for at least a month, so they had better try and find something to do until then.

# Chapter 5

**B**eth soon discovered what Jack was planning to do, and it didn't include her. A week after they had moved in, everything suddenly went very quiet. Dad's holiday time was over and he started back at work. Mum said she wanted to be left in peace to scour the newspaper for jobs. Jack had disappeared upstairs, leaving Beth sitting on the front step hoping to see the builders. But the island was silent. There was no sign of the workmen returning, even though they had left their tools lying around and they still had lots of work to do strengthening the bridge joining the island to Ferry Road.

Beth wondered what to do. Maybe Jack would have an idea. Beth headed up the stairs, knocked on his door then walked in.

Jack's room was, as usual, incredibly tidy. Everything was put away in drawers and he had even made his bed. Planes and things to do with planes were everywhere and Jack had hung his model aircraft from the ceiling on bits of string. He had angled them so that when they moved in the breeze they almost looked as if they were flying.

"Hey, what are you doing? Fancy coming out?"

Jack's response was a grunt. After a few steps forward, Beth could see what he was doing and her heart sank. He had set up his flight simulator game. It was hopeless to try and get any sense out of him now. He was glued to the screen, all his attention focused on attempting to guide his plane on to an aircraft carrier.

It was so boring, Beth thought. She found the game absolutely baffling and her efforts at playing it had quickly ended in disaster.

Conversation proved equally hopeless when Jack was involved in it.

"Do you fancy doing something?" Beth asked.

"I am."

"No, something interesting."

"Huh."

"Come on, it's great out there."

"Huh."

Beth folded her arms. He wasn't even listening. "I've got some money, we could go out on an expedition."

"No, you haven't," Jack replied, still not turning his head. "I might come out, but not till the afternoon. Once I've finished this, I reckon there'll be some planes to spot. It's our turn to get them overhead."

"Oh, great. Be boring then. I'm off." Beth stormed out, her parting shot echoing on the stairs. "What is the point of younger brothers? Get a life."

Beth felt cross, restless and hot. She walked briskly out of the house and on to Ferry Road. Almost without knowing how she had got there, she found herself standing in front of the junk shop. The wooden box was in the window, unmoved and as intriguing as before. "All right then," Beth said aloud. "This is your last chance. I'll try one more time and that's it."

She strode determinedly up the path and tried the handle. To her surprise, it moved. Beth's momentum carried her over the threshold and into the shop. She managed to stop herself before bumping into a dark piece of furniture, stacked high with unsteadily balanced objects. "Ooops, woah, phew," Beth said. Her voice seemed very loud in the cluttered space. "Hello… Anyone there?"

She strained to hear a response while her eyes got used to the murky light. The bright sunlight filtered through the dust on the windows and turned into a soft brown glow. A narrow winding path led between old furniture, boxes, trunks, deck chairs, stuffed animals piled high in every part of the room. The smells of mildew, dust and old leather mingled with each other and swirled around.

"Wow," Beth breathed. What a discovery — this was a real Aladdin's cave.

"Is anyone there?" she repeated.

"Hello dear, can I help you?"

The quiet voice made Beth start. She turned around. Standing in the shadows at the back of the shop was a slight figure. From her voice, Beth could tell that she was a woman, but she was so thin and slightly built that she hardly appeared solid.

"Hello... I, er ... I was just looking. You are open, aren't you?"

"Of course. I'm glad you came in. You timed it just right, I won't be here much longer."

"Oh dear, that's a shame. It's such an interesting shop. I noticed it a week ago. We've just moved — to one of the new houses."

"Yes, dear, I know."

Beth peered at the shopkeeper. She could just make out that she had short hair and she sounded about the same age as her mum. In the room at the back of the shop, Beth heard a faint voice and glimpsed some figures moving around. "I ... er, it's nice and cool in here. I guess that's good for antiques. And it's a nice change from out there."

"Yes, you're right. There hasn't been anything like this for years. Not since the summer of '41."

"Oh, right. You've got lots of wonderful things. Where do they come from?"

"Just locally. It's amazing what you can find if you look. Feel free to browse around."

"Well, thank you. Um, but I think I've already found something I like." Beth pointed down to the object in the window. "I saw it on the first day and thought it looked really interesting."

"You have got good taste. That radio's one of my favourite items too."

"The radio? Of course, I should have known that's what it is."

"It's nice to see people of your age interested in these old things. You do like it, don't you?"

Beth nodded. She ran a hand over the radio's arched top, savouring the cool feel of its smooth surface. Her fingers strayed down over the face, touching chunky buttons and smooth dials.

The owner spoke again. "Would you like to have it? As I said, our time here is nearly over and we can't take these things with us. I know you'll give it a good home."

"Oh, no, I couldn't," Beth replied.

"Please. Think of it as a special offer. You would be making me very happy... That is, unless you don't want it."

"It's not that..."

"Then I insist. Please take it."

"Well, that's very generous of you but I must give you something for it."

"I wouldn't dream of it. You'll be doing me a favour taking it off my hands. I'll just wrap it in newspaper to protect it... There, be careful – it's heavy."

A few seconds later, Beth found herself blinking in the sunlight, clutching the radio in her hands. The sudden contrast from shade to light, from cool to hot, made her feel momentarily giddy. The feeling quickly passed after she took some deep breaths.

Once she felt better, Beth set off down the road. At the end she glanced back. The shop looked as run-down and as empty as ever. In fact it looked as though no one had been inside it for years. If she hadn't been holding the radio, she would have dismissed it all as some sort of hallucination. Beth scratched her head. Maybe she was going soft?

Jack certainly thought so when he saw what she had come home with. "It doesn't even work," he said, laughing. "I hope you didn't pay for this heap of junk."

Beth scowled at him. A quick dusting had brought the radio back to its former glory. The wood glowed with a deep, dark sheen. Beth loved turning the knobs and listening to the satisfying clunk of the on switch, but best of all were the foreign names printed over the wavebands.

Mum and Dad had been more interested in it. "I haven't seen one of these sets since I was your age," Mum told her. "My grandparents used to have one for years before handing it down to me. They told me that during the war they used to spend all their evenings around it listening to the broadcasts."

"Yes, it's a real beauty – a crystal wireless set. It's a shame it doesn't work. You turn it on here, then you'd have to wait for the set to warm up and the light to come on. It's a beautiful object, really well made."

"You see!" Beth sneered at her brother. She waited for the others to leave, then sat on her bed admiring the radio. Beth had known exactly where it should go and it looked perfect in its new position on her dressing table by the window.

Tea was late that evening. Afterwards, Beth ran up to her room and sat in front of the radio. She turned the dial. It stopped at Radio Tangiers, then Radio Paris. At each stop she tried to imagine the sounds that would have come from the long-silent radio stations. After a while she yawned. Outside it was dark. She pulled the curtains and went to bed.

# Chapter 6

Darkness, silence, stillness. Where was she? Pause. Of course, she was in her new room, in Ferry Road. Sigh. What was the time? Instinctively, Beth reached out for her alarm clock. Instead of turning it round, her fingers knocked it off the table.

Blindly she fumbled for it, but her sweeping searches only succeeded in pushing the clock further under the bed. Beth struggled to rise through the layers of deep sleep that enveloped her. Her mind felt muzzy and her eyelids were so heavy that she could hardly lift them. At last she managed to open them a fraction. Blackness greeted them, a darkness that she had never imagined possible. She could see nothing — she could have been floating in outer space for all she knew.

Beth blinked and the effort almost exhausted her. She peered through half-shut eyes. The blackness had been replaced by a thick mist that clouded her vision. After a time the mist changed colour, became lighter. Slowly Beth realized there was a light shining from somewhere, from on her dressing table. It grew brighter, casting a warm, orange glow. The mist cleared for a second and she made out that it was coming from the radio.

*Crackle, hiss.* Static filled the room. Through the electric hiss came voices. The tuning dial moved, the voices changed to music, a trombone here, an oboe there. It was as though an invisible person was trying to find a radio channel. There was a woman singing in a foreign language, a man talking, then on to — no, back again to the man. The dial stopped.

Beth tried to listen. "...*a report on last night's bombing*..." The voice she heard was that of a well-spoken man. "*Enemy planes followed the river ... past our defences ... bombs fell on the city causing damage to buildings...*" It was hard to make out what he was saying. The words faded in and out of earshot and seemed to be coming from far, far away. "*...fires are reported to be burning in the East End but the vigilance of wardens and civilians limited casualties...*"

Slowly the voice died away as the light on the radio faded back into darkness. The mist descended and Beth's eyes closed. She didn't know how long she had been sleeping when she felt herself wake up.

"What's going on?" she murmured drowsily. There was no answer. Beth became aware that she was getting out of bed. She didn't know why – her limbs seemed to be acting on their own as if they were disconnected from her mind.

Suddenly Beth realized that she was standing up by the window. The curtains were open and she was staring out into the night. No street lamps, signs or car headlights pierced the dark for miles. Only in the distance could she see light. Over in the direction of London the sky was glowing orange. Sharp shafts of white light were stabbing up into the blackness.

She could smell the river and hear rain beating against the glass. Dark clouds were racing across the sky. The moon appeared behind them, transforming the river into a glittering silver snake curling towards her. It reflected off the panes of a glass building at the edge of the island. The glasshouse was intact, restored to its former beauty. It was clearly visible, no trees or bushes were growing around it. It lay at the end of a neatly tended garden that led back towards the house. Beth noticed light spilling from downstairs yet their home didn't extend that far out. And what about the other new houses? Where were they? Her gaze was caught by movement. Someone was outside, in their garden. It looked like a girl…

A thick cloud obscured the moon, plunging Beth back into blackness. The mist rose in front of her and her eyes closed.

She woke up in a panic. What was happening? Her brain was spinning. She was outside. It was raining. She was standing in the garden, in the exact spot where she had seen the girl. What was going on? At that moment her ears picked up something – a faint buzzing sound. Suddenly Beth felt a terrible fear – a black alley, dead-end fear. It was like a physical weight that pressed down on her. It invaded her body, leaving her paralysed and helpless. Fear, panic and confusion swept and crashed through her mind.

Beth looked up. A huge shape, like a giant insect, was flying through the sky. She found herself running towards the glasshouse. There was somebody near it. A boy! Beth was shouting but she didn't know what. Her cries broke off as a sudden pain shot through her ankle. She was falling, trees, ground and sky spinning crazily around her. The terrible creature in the sky was almost over her. Four black shapes dropped from its belly. She heard a SPLASH, SPLASH, THUD then

BOOM. In the instant before losing consciousness, Beth saw a red spout burst from the ground. Her body shook as earth, glass and metal flew upwards, then there was nothing.

# Chapter 7

When Beth woke up she found herself lying on her bed. Daylight was filtering in through the curtains, casting an orangey-red glow over the room. As soon as she tried to sit up, a terrible pounding filled her head. She looked around. Her sheets were rumpled and tangled around her and the covers were all over the floor. Shafts of red hot pain shot through her brain. Something had happened last night, but what?

Of course, she had had a dream, a weird dream – and it had felt so real. Snatches of jumbled memory came back. She had been afraid, it had been dark, there was a terrible flash of bright light. There had been more than that, Beth was sure. She knitted her eyebrows together in concentration.

"Think!" she said. "Think hard."

The light. Yes, there had been another light before that blinding flash. Now it was coming back to her. It had come from the radio. The radio had been working! She had heard voices, a broadcast.

Beth got out of bed and reached out to click the on button. Nothing. CLICK ON, CLICK OFF, CLICK ON. Still nothing. The radio was dead. Beth shook her head. What else did she expect? It had just been a dream. Of course the radio wouldn't work now.

Beth sighed. She looked absent-mindedly out of the window. The view jolted her memory. Last night she had done the same thing in her dream. But what had she seen? It was all so hazy. She knew it was important to remember. Her brain held the answer but as soon as she got close it slipped away. She tried even harder. Eventually some of the details began to return. Yes, it was becoming clearer.

That was it. She had been outside in a storm … and … and there had been some noises. A splash, splash, thud and then a loud boom! Beth shivered.

BANG, BANG. The knock on the door made Beth jump. It creaked open and Mum's head appeared.

"Good heavens, what a mess!" she exclaimed. "What have you been doing in here? It looks like a bomb's hit it."

"Oh, er, nothing," replied Beth, patting down some of her hair that was sticking out at all angles. She looked at her room. The neatness of that first day hadn't lasted and soon things had reverted to their normal, comfortable state. As the bedclothes were in a state of total chaos, strewn about all over the floor, too, Beth supposed that Mum might have a point.

Mum looked at her curiously. "Hmmm, well, if you say so. I was just popping in to say that I'm leaving with your father today. I've got a job interview and I'm going to drop him off on the way. We'll be going in a few minutes so you'll have to get your own breakfast, OK?" Beth nodded. "And look after your brother. I don't want you two playing down by the river, is that understood?"

Beth nodded again. "And I expect this room to be tidy when I come back. There'll be an inspection."

Beth groaned inwardly. "All right, and good luck... Oh, er, I was just wondering. You didn't hear anything, well anything go, sort of bang, in the night, did you?"

Mum smiled. "This isn't one of your famous burglar alarms, is it?" she asked. "Like that time you heard noises and convinced us that there were burglars outside. I don't know where you got that cricket bat for Dad. We turned the light on just in time to stop him knocking a squirrel for six."

"Actually, it was a hedgehog," Beth muttered, her ears burning with embarrassment. It wasn't fair. She had made one simple, honest, mistake and it had gone down in the annals of family history for ever – much to everyone else's continued amusement.

"Oh, dear," Mum grinned. "That was funny. But to answer your question – no, we didn't hear anything. Why?"

"It doesn't really matter," came Beth's cross reply. "I just had a dream last night, it was raining and there was a loud sort of bang in it. I wondered if there had been a storm last night or something. You know, I could have heard thunder and put it in my dream."

"No, it was a fine night," said Mum. Still chuckling, she shut the door.

Typical, Beth thought. Still, that would teach her not to get too worried. It had obviously just been a very real, very strange dream. She wouldn't think about it again. And anyway, now she had the room to tidy up.

Beth groaned. Cleaning up was not her idea of having a good time. She plonked herself down on the bed – she needed to gather her energy together first.

I know, I'll tidy up as much as I can while lying in bed, she thought. The idea cheered Beth up. She leaned over the edge of the bed to pick up a pillow that had fallen on the floor.

Underneath it was her alarm clock. So I did really knock it off the table, she thought. That's odd.

And there had been something odd in her dream too. Beth was sure she had seen some sort of huge shape flying in the sky. She had thought it was a giant insect. "Yeuch!" she shuddered. That just went to prove what a weird dream it had been. Her imagination had obviously been running riot. It was definitely best forgotten about.

It was a good idea but Beth found it more difficult than she thought. As hard as she tried to put the dream out of her mind, snatches of it kept crowding in on her. Beth decided that she needed distracting. Tidying up certainly wasn't helping – and nor did breakfast. Eventually, Beth found herself knocking on Jack's door.

"Morning, Jack. How are you?"

"I'm all right."

"Would you like breakfast? There's loads of stuff in."

"No, ta. I had some before you were up."

"Oh, well, if you're sure. There's nothing I can bring you?"

"Look, Beth. What do you want?"

"What do you mean?"

"What I said. What do you want? You're being far too nice, you must want something."

Beth crossed her arms and tried to look hurt. "That's gratitude for you. I just came in for a chat. So what are you doing?"

"I'm spotting, if you want to know. I've already seen a 737 and an airbus."

"How interesting," Beth said, stifling a yawn. "Have you been out yet? It's a beautiful day. I thought we could…"

She didn't finish the sentence. At that moment Jack interrupted her by clambering on to the window sill. "There's one coming down really low. I've worked out that the planes only come overhead on their good weather flight-path. They have different routes depending on wind speed and direction as well as weather. The only problem is that I can't really see them from here, I need to be outside." And with that, Jack hared off downstairs.

Beth followed. She stepped outside to see her brother staring up at a plane as it flew low overhead. For at least a minute she could see it in surprising close-up with its shiny, brightly painted tail and its wheels locked down for a landing.

"Not bad, eh?" said Jack, above the roar of the engines. Beth brushed the loose lock of hair out of her eyes and grunted – she had to admit it was quite an impressive sight, although it was very noisy.

The plane disappeared over the rooftops towards the airport. Reluctantly Jack turned his gaze away. "You get a much better view from here than from my room, you know. Oh, well, I think that'll be the last one over us for a while. Seeing as we're here, how about doing something? A game of frisbee?"

Beth nodded. It was a good suggestion. She enjoyed playing the game while Jack was always eager to show off his latest special throws. There was only one problem: where was the frisbee?

They spent twenty hot, frustrating minutes

sorting through dusty boxes in the shed until Beth remembered where it might be. She was sure Dad had packed it in with their picnic things in the kitchen.

She was right. Jack spotted the bright yellow saucer once they tipped out the cool bag. They picked their way through a mass of plastic plates, cups and cutlery on the kitchen floor and went back outside.

"What about the front?" asked Jack.

Beth shook her head. The area at the front of the house was too small and there were piles of bricks and cement bags lying around. Instead they chased each other round to the back of the house. Although there were some plants in the flowerbeds, no fences had been put up around any of the other gardens so they had much more space. Beth turned her head and could see sunlight reflecting off her bedroom window.

"Let's go," she said. "First one to drop it has to tidy the bedrooms."

Beth waited for Jack to nod his agreement, then started with an easy loosener. Jack caught and returned it in one easy motion. The game continued with each player running and jumping, using the wind to send the small plastic saucer soaring between them. Beth spun it on one finger then threw a looping, spinning shot to her brother. Jack returned it with a skimmer that stayed just above the ground, stinging Beth's fingers as she plucked it out of the air.

"Oww," gasped Beth.

Her brother grinned. "You need some practice," he yelled.

"All right," Beth muttered under her breath. "I'll show you who needs practice." She felt the sharp rim under her fingers. "Now!" Quick as a flash, she whipped back her wrist and let go. The frisbee fizzed through the air. It looked as though it was about to hit the ground in front of Jack, then it lifted up and flew through his fingers.

Beth burst out laughing at the surprised look on his face. "What did you say about practice? You can think about that while you're doing the tidying up. But I think you'd better get the frisbee back first."

Still smiling, she turned her back on Jack's complaints and sat down in the sun. She squinted up into the sky. Wispy clouds were spread out over the sky, making a pattern like surf crashing on a beach. Beth tilted her head to see if they made any other shapes. After a while she got bored and looked around for Jack. Where was he? He had been gone a long time.

"Come on, little brother. Quit playing around. I was joking, that's all. Let's carry on with the game."

No response. Beth tried again. Again there was no reply. Annoyance showed in two red spots on her cheeks, but it swiftly changed to concern. Even Jack should have been getting fed up with the joke by now – unless he wasn't playing a joke.

Beth started to her feet. Jack had gone off to fetch the frisbee. The last time she had seen it, it had been heading towards the copse of trees and bushes near the river bank.

All of a sudden she remembered what the copse hid – the ruined glasshouse! She had been so busy and there had been so many distractions during their first week that she had forgotten all about it since that first sighting. She remembered that it had appeared in her dream last night, only it hadn't been a ruin then, it had been intact. Beth felt a surge of panic, even dread, rise up in her. She had experienced the same feeling before – in the dream.

Pull yourself together, she urged herself. This was no time to be stupid. What on earth was there to be scared about? With one last shout to check that Jack was not around, Beth plucked up her courage and plunged into the green foliage. A few steps later she looked over her shoulder. She could scarcely see the house or where she and Jack had been playing – she had been swallowed up by the trees.

Beth strode on. Branches lashed out at her and roots hidden in the undergrowth nipped at her ankles. The going got tougher as the foliage got denser. Beth had to crouch down low but still branches whipped at her and leaves slapped her in the face. It was almost as though they were trying to stop her getting through the copse. She felt herself getting hotter and more flustered by the minute. A cobweb clung uncomfortably to her hair. When she tried to untangle the sticky strands she shrieked as she felt a spider crawl over her hands then spin down to the ground, unspooling more sticky silk as it went.

"Owww!" Beth spun round and banged her head on a branch. Dizzily, she tried to stand up straight and to recover her poise. She brushed her hair back from her face. She was in a small clearing. All around were trees and bushes. She couldn't see the house or the river. Surely she couldn't be lost, the copse wasn't that big. And yet, and yet… She felt so small and disorientated. She felt alone and cut off, as though entering the copse was like stepping into another place, or even another time.

"Jack!" Beth's shout bounced off the trees and was flung back at her, sounding more like a desperate cry than the angry call it was meant to be. She strained her ears for a response.

What was that? Beth waited. There it came again. She wasn't imagining it, she could hear voices and the sound of footsteps running through the trees. She ran towards the noises but as soon as she got close they faded away. "Who's there?" Beth's attempt at decisiveness once again failed miserably. "Jack, I'm not impressed by this game. Come on out."

Again whispers floated through the air. They were coming from a few metres away. She dashed towards them, only for them to fade into silence. A few seconds later she heard them once again. They were coming from behind a thick bush. She stood still, listening. They were too quiet for the words to be made out. It was like trying to catch leaves on a windy autumn day – just when she thought she was about to grab them, they drifted away.

Whoever was talking was moving away. Always just behind, Beth followed the sound of the voices. In the dappled sunlight she thought she could make out something moving. Was that the shadow of a person she could see flitting between the trees or was she imagining it?

Of course it had to be a person, Beth thought. And if she looked closely she would probably see another. Although she couldn't hear what was being said, she made out two voices, one male and one female.

"Hey," she shouted. "Will you stop a minute? Stop."

At that moment the voices died away altogether. Beth carried on a few steps and, to her amazement, found herself stepping out of the trees into bright sunlight. She was out of the copse, home was directly ahead. A feeling of relief, of happiness washed over her. The voices had led her out of the copse. But where were the people who had been talking? There was no sign of them. Beth looked around. And what about Jack? She couldn't see him — he must still be in the copse.

Beth turned on her heels. She had to find Jack. Through the trees she crashed. Hold on, what was that? She saw someone moving — was it Jack? She couldn't be sure. The harder she tried, the harder it was to get a good look. The light was playing tricks on her eyes – it almost seemed to be shining *through* the smallish figure ahead.

"Hey, wait for me," she said. The figure moved soundlessly, as Beth crashed clumsily behind. Suddenly she was out of the copse and beside the river. She saw Jack standing a few paces away, his back turned to her.

She covered the distance in three long strides. "OK, I think that's enough of this stupid game," she shouted, stretching out her hand.

To her amazement, she touched nothing. The only sensation she felt was a blast of cold air freezing her hand. She tried to regain her balance but her feet lost their grip and she crashed to the floor.

Beth turned over and looked up. She found herself staring up at two children. One of them was the boy she had thought was Jack. He did look just like Jack, although her brother would never wear the grey baggy shorts that the boy had on. He had been joined by a girl. She was the same age as Beth and had the same untidy black hair. She was wearing a pretty summer dress with a school blazer over the top. But what really caught Beth's attention was that the two children were so pale, their faces deathly white.

The pair moved towards her. They made no sound, as if they were gliding above the ground. The temperature seemed to have dropped. Beth shivered and tried to back away – to no avail. She was rooted to the spot, trapped. It felt as though an invisible force was gripping her. The children came closer. The girl's mouth moved. A word carried over to her: "Danger! Danger! Danger!" The word was repeated and got stronger, imprinting itself on Beth's brain.

What danger? What did they want? Beth could only watch as the girl opposite slowly raised her head. Beth gasped. The girl's eyes held pools of such sadness that Beth felt she would cry.

"Go away, get away from me!" At last Beth found her voice. The spell was broken. She got to her feet and tried to escape back into the copse. She had only taken a few steps before a figure appeared, blocking her path. It was too late to dodge. Beth let out a strangled shriek before *crunch*, she felt herself hit a surprisingly solid person.

# Chapter 8

"Where did you spring from? You ought to be more careful, running around crazily like that."

Beth lay winded on the ground. She looked up at the person who had appeared in her path. It was the old man from Ferry Road. Beth had time to look at him a bit more closely now. His white hair was uncombed and straggled down over his collar. Greying stubble was growing around his chin. He was wearing a dirty shirt with rolled-up sleeves revealing beefy forearms that were covered in tattoos. His fingers were thick too, with grubby, broken nails. Making no attempt to help, he folded his arms and stared at Beth.

"So, it's you again, is it? Well, what are you doing here? Do your parents let you attack old people like this?"

Beth edged away from the man. She was feeling terribly confused. Her encounter with the two strange children had really shaken her and now this. Slowly, her breath returned in short painful gulps. She managed to get her thoughts into order. "I wasn't attacking you. I was … well, I was… Have you seen any other children around here?"

As if on cue, Jack appeared. "Hello, Beth. Oh, I see you've met, er, this man. I don't want to sound silly, but what are you doing down there?"

"She leapt out of the bushes at me and got more than she bargained for. You kids shouldn't be out here menacing innocent folks who are minding their own business. I've told you that already. First that plastic thing almost takes my head off and then she tries to finish the job."

Beth waved Jack's hand away and got to her feet crossly. Ignoring the man's rudeness, she answered Jack's question. "I was trying to find you, actually. What do you think you were playing at? You were supposed to be bringing back the frisbee, remember? Not gallivanting around by the river."

"OK, OK. But I did get it. This man gave it to me. It flew into the trees here and when I was trying to find it, I discovered this brilliant place. There's a ruined building just along from here. I'm going to make it my secret hide-out – it'll be great for plane spotting. I can see them much better from here."

Beth glanced over Jack's shoulder. Through the trees she could see the skeleton of the glasshouse. She shivered. A deadly quiet hung over the area. The smell of stagnant water and moss filled the air. Damp and neglect were everywhere.

Beth felt a terrible sadness rise up and form a lump in her throat. She pictured with startling clearness how beautiful the glasshouse must have been. But now red rust stained the iron supports like blood and the interior was choked with weeds and stinging nettles. Clouds of midges swarmed above the crater-like inlet where the river lapped against the shore. A plastic cup and a fizzy drinks bottle were visible above the scummy surface of the brown water. It certainly didn't look like a great place to her – and the old man seemed to agree.

"Aye, that's where I found the young rascal – vandalizing property! I told him then and I'll tell you now. If you're wise you'll take my advice and not come down to this part of the river again. It's not safe, do you hear?"

Beth nodded. She certainly didn't want to come back here – she might see those two children again. They had given her a real fright. They had been so strange ... so ghostly. Get a grip, Beth thought. She was letting her imagination run away with her. Before she could order her thoughts, the man spoke again.

"I take it that you've found who you were looking for. Unless there are some more of you causing mischief?"

"I'm sure Jack wasn't doing any harm,"

replied Beth. "The only ones doing mischief are the other two," she muttered.

"What two?"

"There were two children. A boy and a girl. About our age. They were back there. Did you see them too?"

Beth's words had a surprising effect on the man. The expression in his voice changed and so did the colour in his cheeks. "No, no. I didn't see them," he said falteringly.

Jack was listening in amazement at the strange turn in the conversation. "Would you mind telling me what's going on?" he asked.

Beth repeated what she had said, giving the man time to recover. "What a lot of nonsense. There are no other children around here," he spluttered. "Don't you forget what I told you. It's not safe around here. If you know what's good for you, you'll not come to this part of the island. Have you got that? Well, I haven't got any more time to talk to a couple of kids, I'm off." With that, he turned abruptly and limped off through the trees.

Jack broke the silence. "What a loon! What was he babbling on about?"

Beth pursed her lips. She didn't know what to think. She was beginning to get used to the man's rudeness but there was still something peculiar about him. He had been very keen on warning them away from the area and her mention of the two children seemed to really shock him. She wondered why.

"Who are these kids you were talking about? I haven't seen any. Do you think they're new neighbours? Let's explore the glasshouse, then we can show it to them."

Jack's suggestion jolted Beth out of her thoughts. She was becoming increasingly sure that for some reason, she should keep Jack away from the glasshouse. "Hold on a second. What *is* the time?" She glanced down at her watch. Their mum was due home and Beth remembered her dreaded last words – bedroom inspection. She also remembered the mess they had left in the kitchen. They had better get back or they would be in trouble.

She dragged Jack reluctantly away from the river bank and headed back towards their house. To Beth's amazement, it only took a couple of minutes before they were through the copse and nearing their front door. There, in the drive was the car. Beth's heart sank — they had been beaten back.

# Chapter 9

"Where do you think you've been?" Beth stared at the floor, cheeks reddening.

"I don't know, I can't believe it. I ask you to do one little thing for me and this is what I find." Beth's mum pointed to the collection of items on the kitchen floor. "I thought you'd know better, especially at your age."

Inside Beth was boiling. It just wasn't fair. It was Jack's fault. If he hadn't gone off and got so excited by the glasshouse, they would have been back in time to tidy things up. It was obvious that the job interview hadn't gone well and Mum's mood had not been improved when she saw Beth's bedroom. Of course, Jack's had been neat and tidy, as always. Beth thought she could cheerfully ring the little creep's neck. She looked out under her eyebrows at him.

"We're sorry about the mess," he said. "It's just that we got distracted. We were down by the river's edge and … oww!"

Beth's swift kick under the table stopped Jack in mid-flow but it was too late. Mum looked sharply at the two of them. "I thought we had made it plain that we don't want you playing by the river. You may think we're being silly and I know you can both swim but the river is a dangerous place. I suppose it was too much for Jack to take it in but I thought you might have stopped him, Beth. Have you got anything to say?"

Beth shrugged her shoulders. She had learned it was best to stay quiet in these situations.

"I thought not. All right then, go and tidy up while your brother sorts out the mess down here – and no complaining."

With a backwards glance into the kitchen, Beth trudged up the stairs and slammed the door behind her. Thoughts of revenge went through her mind as she thought about Jack and his big mouth. Well, that would teach her to play stupid games with him. She stared at her room in despair. It would take hours to clear up. Why did parents have this thing about tidiness? She screwed up a sheet of yellowing newspaper and aimed it at the bin. It missed.

"Typical," groaned Beth, throwing herself on her bed. Moodily, she began to gather up armfuls of clothes, ready to stuff them into drawers. The room became gradually tidier and slowly Beth began to order her thoughts. She couldn't escape the feeling that something strange was going on. First there had been that weird dream and then the strange business down by the glasshouse. The old man was bad enough but it was those children who had really spooked her. Surely they couldn't be what she had thought? Sitting in her room in the sunshine, it was hard to believe that she might have seen ghosts. Was her imagination running away with her again? The last time she had thought she'd seen a ghost, it had been Jack. Could it have just been a trick of the light that made them look so pale?

Beth scratched her head. Should she tell Jack about her worries? What would he say? A sudden memory sprang into her head. On her first day she had seen two figures near the glasshouse. They must have been the two children. What were they doing by the glasshouse? Indeed, what was a ruined glasshouse doing on the island? Maybe it concealed some clues and she should investigate it.

Beth shivered at the thought. No way, the place gave her the creeps. It was dangerous too. That was what the two children had said to her. *They* were the danger, Beth decided. She certainly didn't want to go there on her own. That would be a last resort. There had to be something else…

Her head was beginning to spin. She closed her eyes. She didn't know how long she had been lying there when she heard a couple of knocks on the door and saw her brother's head peering around it.

"Hi. I think Mum's calmed down a bit. I thought I'd better warn you that she'll be coming up soon – do you want a hand tidying?"

Beth recognized a peace offering when she heard one. Still, she let him stew for a few moments before nodding. There wasn't really anything to do, but she did want to talk to Jack about what had happened, just to see what he thought.

Beth's room passed the inspection with flying colours. To show how pleased she was, Mum allowed Jack and Beth to make her some tea. Beth closed the kitchen door but it was Jack who got the first words in.

"So what do you think of my idea of making a den in the ruined glasshouse?" asked Jack eagerly. "All it needs is a bit of work, then it'll be perfect. I might even persuade the olds to let me camp out there overnight. What do you think?"

Beth knew what she thought but she didn't

know how to tell Jack. "I don't like it down there," she began. "There's a funny atmosphere – it's creepy. Haven't you noticed it?"

"I suppose it's a bit damp and a bit cold, but that's because it's by the river."

"No, it's more than that. There was that man for a start."

"Surely you didn't pay any attention to him! He's just a grumpy old bloke."

"Yes, perhaps..." Beth hesitated for a minute then she plunged in. "It's not only him though... I saw two children down there. There was something strange about them and they just seemed to vanish."

Jack shrugged. "Oh, come on. The trees are thick around there, they probably just walked away and were hidden by them. I don't know why you're making a big deal out of it."

"Well, I just ... I mean, who were they? What were they doing there?"

"It's like I said, they might have been looking around the houses with their parents. Or they could be local kids who've found the place."

"I don't think so. I didn't notice anyone looking at the houses and we haven't seen anyone else our age around here. They were... It was just strange."

"So what's the big deal? Come on, you'll be telling me that you thought they were ghosts next."

Beth looked him in the eye. Jack laughed. "That's ridiculous. You're imagining things again. Like the time when you thought we had burglars and it turned out to be a fox. We only just stopped Dad in time. Otherwise he'd have been in trouble with the RSPCA."

"It was a hedgehog, actually. And I'm not imagining things, as you reckon."

"Leave it out," came the reply. "Of course they weren't ghosts. I know, you're just jealous because I found the den first and you're trying to scare me off. Well, it won't work. You can't fool me. I know you don't get ghosts, not in broad daylight. Ghosts wail or jangle chains in haunted houses, they don't hang out in a greenhouse by the river."

"Not unless they had a good reason to be there."

"Like what? Like they're keen gardeners, or maybe they got eaten by a man-eating tropical plant? Come on, Beth, do me a favour. They're just normal kids. It's not haunted, just look around. I can't think of anywhere less likely to have ghosts than here."

Beth found herself reluctantly agreeing. From the kitchen window they could see over the bridge and down Ferry Road. The glasshouse was safely out of sight while the street ahead looked safe and familiar. Various people were going about their everyday tasks in a quiet, unhurried way. Beth spotted Mr White putting oranges into a customer's basket, a couple of people chatting outside the newsagent's, a cyclist slowly pedalling away from the baker's. Jack was right, she was being silly. And yet ... and yet, she couldn't ignore her instincts.

What about the old man? He was definitely real. What had he been doing by the glasshouse and why had he behaved so strangely? While Beth turned off the kettle and filled the teapot, she made some decisions. If she happened to find herself at the shops she would ask a few discreet questions about him – and maybe about the children too. Jack was right, they were probably just local kids and somebody would know about them. She was sure the questions wouldn't lead anywhere, it was just to reassure herself...

Jack's loud chuckle burst through her thoughts. "You know, you're the only strange thing going on around here. I don't know how you do it, I don't know how you manage to get more tea over your T-shirt than in the mug, but you just have. Maybe these ghosties have cursed you. I think you'd better keep your eye out for killer teapots instead of imaginary ghouls."

Beth groaned. Jack was right. She had been so deep in thought that she had overpoured the mug and it had spilled all over her top. She wiped the bottom of the mug and followed Jack, who was carrying the biscuits. Beth put the tea down next to Mum's chair, then made to go upstairs.

"Beth, what have you done to that shirt? Where are you going?"

"I've got to change. I know you wouldn't want me to go out wearing this."

"You're right," came the reply. "But you're not going anywhere today. You're grounded – both of you – for the rest of the day. I've got a few jobs for you to do. Don't worry though, you can change first."

The tone of Mum's voice brooked no argument. Beth stomped dejectedly upstairs, wondering what jobs Mum had got planned for them.

# Chapter 10

The next day dawned even hotter than the ones before. Beth chose her lightest T-shirt and shorts to wear and went downstairs. Over the sound of Jack munching his toast, the radio was reporting hose-pipe bans and was full of stories about tarmac melting on motorways and people fainting at cricket matches.

After breakfast, Mum asked for a volunteer to buy bread. Of course Jack wasn't interested. For some reason he said he would help Mum with the washing up and as a result Beth found herself volunteered. She left the house while Jack was asking Mum about some sort of DIY plans, and decided to take the opportunity to ask some questions.

She wandered past the shop where she had been given the radio. She had thought of going in and asking the owner about the old man and the children but if anything the shop looked even more deserted and unused than before. Beth had no luck at her first stop. The news-agent shook her head at her questions about the children, so Beth left and tried the bakery.

The shop was empty when she went in. The baker seemed pleased to see her but again her questions about the children met with a blank look. Beth decided to try and ask about the old man but first she remembered she had some shopping to do.

"Could I have a loaf of bread, please?" she asked.

"Certainly. This one? Yes? I hope we'll be seeing you on Sunday – at the fête."

Beth was puzzled. "What fête?"

"The Ferry Road Fête. Surely you've seen the signs. Here's a leaflet."

Beth read the proffered leaflet. "Our annual

fête will take place on 25th August. All are welcome. BBQ, tombola, raffle, cakes and a coconut shy. The fun begins at 1:30 – don't be late."

"Oh, I'm sure we'll be there. It sounds great."

"It will be. You must come – it's a real tradition around here. This will be the 120th fête. My family have been organizing it for decades. There's a great deal of work of course, but I don't mind. I like to get everything planned out in advance. It's very important to approach it all methodically. We don't want any last minute surprises – you'd be amazed at what can go wrong."

"Yes, I'm sure I would." Beth managed to interrupt the flow of words briefly.

"Well, I mustn't go on about things going wrong. I'm sure everything will go off splendidly. And of course it's a great way to meet all your neighbours. All the local people come as well as others from miles away."

"That's interesting. I suppose all your regulars will be there. I've already met a few of them. There's one in particular. I don't know his name. He's got white hair, big build, a tattoo on his arm…"

"That can only be Bill – Bill Barnes. He's not upset you, has he?"

"Oh, no," lied Beth. This Bill Barnes was obviously well known. "I've just bumped into him a few times and he seems interesting."

"That's one word to describe him, although I've heard a few others that I wouldn't like to repeat. He's a real loner. He doesn't seem to like people very much – or the fête. I've never seen him there. He used to be the ferryman. There are ferry rights across the river here and there used to be a regular crossing. Did you know that?"

Beth shook her head, slowly taking in what the baker said. She had never thought that Ferry Road might actually be named after a ferry crossing.

The baker smiled and continued, "It dates back to Henry the Eighth. There used to be a racecourse on the other side of the river. Quite famous it was – I think Dickens mentioned it in one of his books. Anyway, the Barnes family had been given the rights to the crossing and they were all ferrymen. But the Second World War put paid to the races. That just left a few daytrippers and the family on your island – not enough to keep the business going. That was before my time, of course. It was Dad who told me about Bill. Anyway, once the ferrying business collapsed, Bill didn't know what else to do. He started drinking too much. In all my years here I've never seen him on the river."

The baker handed Beth her loaf. "If you want to know more about it you could do worse than ask Reg – the greengrocer. Bill was great friends with Reg's dad in his youth although I think they had a falling out. He might be able to tell you some more."

"I will, thanks!"

Beth pondered what she had found out on her way to the grocer's. Bill Barnes obviously had quite an interesting past – a ferryman indeed.

"Loverly, jubberly, what can I do you for,

madam? Lov-er-ly ripe peaches 'ere."

Beth had reached the greengrocer's. "No, thanks," she said. "Mum bought a load of fruit yesterday. Actually, I've come from Mr Stevens. He suggested that you might be able to help me with some questions."

"Fire away – Reg White's always pleased to be of service."

"Thank you. Um, we were just talking about Bill Barnes. And he said you knew him well."

The greengrocer chuckled. "I should say so. Old Bill Barnes. Everyone's been on the sharp end of his tongue once in their life. It's a shame really, he was supposed to be a totally different character when he was young. He used to be great friends with my father. They were a right couple of rogues by all accounts. You know – they did a bit of ducking and diving."

"But they fell out, didn't they? That's what Mr Stevens said. Did they have an argument?"

"I'm not sure really. It was all a bit

mysterious. You see, my dad died in the war when I was young and it was my mum who mentioned it. There was one thing that I do remember though. She told me that Bill had sworn never to go on the river again. And as far as I know, he never has."

Beth frowned. Bill Barnes was getting more interesting by the minute. She wondered what had caused the falling out between him and the greengrocer's dad. And as for the last piece of news, what would make a ferryman swear never to go out on the river again?

The greengrocer tapped her on the shoulder. "If you find out why, I'd like to know the answer," he said. "Anyway, now's your chance to talk him, he's over there."

Beth looked up and spotted Bill Barnes on the other side of the road. Mr White was right. Why shouldn't she go up and talk to him? So what if he had a sharp tongue? Beth was prepared for him this time. She would just take care not to surprise him.

By the time Beth had decided that she would talk to him, Bill Barnes had walked past her. With a parting wave, she left Mr White and hurried across the road.

The ex-ferryman moved with surprising speed despite his limp. Beth lengthened her stride in an attempt to make up lost ground. Heat was bouncing off the pavement and Beth felt sweat break out on her forehead. Up ahead, Mr Barnes paused and looked over his shoulder. Some instinct made Beth duck behind a car. She looked beneath the tyres and saw a pair of feet turn left into an alley between two cottages.

"I've never seen this before," Beth thought, skirting the car and following the ferryman. Her relief at being out of the sun evaporated when she saw the alley was empty. She broke into a trot. At the end of the narrow passage she saw a rough stone path that led along the river and was overgrown with thick bushes. She looked in both directions. Where was Bill Barnes? A branch moving betrayed his position. Beth narrowed her eyes as she saw him stop by the door of a battered wooden building. He looked around furtively before scuttling quickly inside. The door closed behind him with a creak.

"Is this where he lives?" Beth wondered. She bit her lip, her footsteps slowing. Was her nerve going? There was something about Bill Barnes' behaviour that had struck her as odd, as if he didn't want anyone to follow him.

Beth clenched her fist – she wasn't going to let herself be scared by a grumpy old man. "Hello!" Her voice didn't sound quite as confident as Beth had intended. Her faint call received no answer.

She took a deep breath and knocked on the door. To her surprise, it creaked open under the pressure of her knuckles. The first thing that struck her was the smell – old river water mixed with diesel oil and grease. Inside was dark as well as dank. Sunlight was coming in through gaps in the roof, only to be blocked and weakened by the wooden roof supports. In the black space in front of her she could hear water lapping and slithering around.

The building wasn't just *by* the water, she realized – it was *on* the water. It was a boathouse! She tiptoed inside, feet searching for a safe foothold on the rickety, warped floorboards. She dodged past a wall that loomed up at her and found herself in the main part of the boathouse.

At the end of the building, the river was bathed in bright sunlight. It bounced off the water and into the boathouse, making patterns on the walls. And there, right in front of her, was a boat – a long, elegant rowing boat. In contrast to its surroundings, the boat was in superb condition. Its bows gleamed with fresh paint and the rowlocks glistened with a thick layer of oil. Kneeling beside it was Bill Barnes.

Wild thoughts swarmed through Beth's head. Why did the ferryman keep a boat when he never went out on the river? Was he a smuggler? As he began lovingly polishing the metalwork, his face was clearly visible. Beth saw his expression of wistful sadness. Suddenly she began to feel self-conscious and guilty. She was intruding on private property and on private feelings. All thoughts of asking questions disappeared. She stepped back blindly, knocking over a metal pot.

The rattling sound broke the silence. Bill Barnes looked up. "Who's there?" he yelled. "Who's that? Come out of there."

Beth heard his calls but she was already out of the boathouse. Without pausing for breath, she fled down the path, heading for home.

# Chapter 11

Beth raced all the way back to the house, only stopping a few steps from the front door to get her breath back and to look over her shoulder. She sighed with relief – there was no sign of the ferryman behind her. With one hand she wiped her brow while with the other she began a fruitless attempt to force her hair back into its band. Her heartbeat was beginning to return to normal when Jack's sudden appearance from the garage startled her.

"Hello. Where've you been? You look a right mess."

"Do I? Thanks. I haven't been anywhere in particular."

"If you say so. Anyway, Mum's looking for you."

"I'll go on in and find her. What were you doing in the garage, by the way?"

"Oh, nothing. Just checking some things. What's that stuff on your trainers?"

Beth looked down. Her right shoe and sock were stained with spots of a black liquid that looked suspiciously like oil. "Oh, no," she groaned. It must have been an oil can she had knocked over in the boathouse. Her mind flashed back to Bill Barnes and his boat, but she had no time to think through what she had seen because just then she heard footsteps from inside the house. She just had time to kick off her trainers before Mum appeared at the door.

"So there you are. I don't know, you both disappear when I want you. No doubt you're engaged in some secret adventures. Well…?"

Both Beth and Jack looked nervously at the ground. They were reassured when Mum continued, "It's all right, I was only joking.

Come on in. It's lunchtime. Have you got that loaf, Beth?"

Ooops. The bread. Where was it? She looked sheepish and held out her empty hands. "I ... I don't know what I did with it. I was chatting and must have left it somewhere. Sorry."

"Really, Beth, I don't know what's got into you the last few days. I never thought you'd be so absent-minded and unreliable. We'll just have to manage without."

As a result of the lost loaf, lunch was a subdued and rather small affair. Both Beth and her brother were deep in their own thoughts. Eventually Mum broke the silence with some good news. She had rung Gran and she would be coming down to see them. She was due to arrive late tomorrow afternoon.

"That's great," Beth said. "Gran'll be here in time to come with us to the Ferry Road Fête. It's happening on Sunday. I've got a leaflet, look!"

Jack and Mum examined the piece of paper Beth had produced. "This sounds like fun," Mum agreed. "At least your shopping trip wasn't completely wasted. OK, you can get down now if you've finished. I'll do the washing up. I don't trust either of you in the moods you're in."

Jack stayed behind to ask about torch batteries while Beth took her chance to leave. She had better try and get the oil off her trainers before Mum noticed. While she was doing that, she would try and think through what she had discovered about Bill Barnes.

In the garage she found an old rag. Unfortunately her attempts at rubbing the oil off her shoe with it only succeeded in spreading the sticky black stain. She needed water but Mum was still in the kitchen.

Moments later Beth came up with a solution. She set off for the river, trainer and rag in one hand. She chose a spot out of sight of home where she could reach down and dip the rag into the water.

Even with the water, cleaning her shoe proved to be hard work. Beth rubbed and rubbed away until she had worked up a sweat. The sun was beating down on her neck and her T-shirt was sticking uncomfortably to her back. She put her trainer down, hoping for a cool breeze to refresh her thoughts.

Although she had drawn a blank with the children, at least she had found out lots of interesting things about Bill Barnes. The only problem was that they all seemed to lead to more questions. Beth sighed. Why had he fallen out with his old friend? Why did he keep a boat when he had sworn never to go out on the river? Why had he sworn never to go on the river in the first place?

Beth laughed sourly. She had thought Bill Barnes might be a smuggler. Who had ever heard of a seventy-year-old smuggler? It was ridiculous. As usual she was getting carried away. It was like the two children. She was trying to make up some mystery where none existed. There were probably simple straight-forward answers to all her questions. She'd be better off forgetting the whole thing.

"Ghosts, mysterious ferrymen – hah! It's stupid." Beth decided to go home and forget about the whole silly business.

She hopped around, putting on her trainer. It wasn't brilliantly clean but it would have to do. Halfway back to the house, she skirted past the copse. A cool breeze caused goose-bumps to appear on her arm. A leaf rustled. A soft whisper carried through the air.

"Danger! Danger!"

Beth froze as the words floated towards her. Once again she felt a moment of panic, of fear, of dread. There, standing in the bushes, were the two children. She felt her eyes being drawn to those terrible white faces. Danger! Beth knew all about that. These ghostly children were dangerous, that was a fact.

"Go away. Leave me alone!" The words choked out of Beth. She turned and ran blindly. She had only taken a few steps when her foot hit something hard, something solid. Beth lost her balance and with a shriek, crashed to the ground. She got to her feet as quickly as she could and glanced fearfully over her shoulder.

Her eyes opened wide in amazement. The two children had vanished without trace. Beth checked around in all directions. Had they really gone? Had they ever been there? Beth swallowed hard, her hands shaking. She darted glances around. Questions crowded into her thoughts. Had she been right about the children or was she going mad?

While she tried to clear a way through her muddled thoughts, her fingers tugged nervously at the ivy growing over the bricks she was sitting on. A long strand came away in her hand. To her surprise, Beth realized that she had uncovered more than just some old bricks. She saw that she was sitting on a gatepost, the sort that stood at the front of grand old houses.

Beth's brain began to race. The gateposts must have marked the site of an old house. An old house that stood on the island! Things were beginning to click into place. Beth vaguely remembered something that the baker had said. What was it exactly now? That was it. He had mentioned that after the races closed down, the only passengers the ferryman had left were a few daytrippers and "the family on your island".

Beth thought hard. He must have meant that a family used to live on this island. They must have lived in a house, and that explained the glasshouse. It would have been built in the grounds of the house on the island.

At last she was getting somewhere. Beth stood up. She spotted some letters, half-obscured by spiders' webs and worn down by wind and rain, that were carved in the gate-post.

"Riv … Rivers…" What were the last few letters? There was an "e" at the end and could that be a "d"? That was it, she'd got it – "Riverside".

"Riverside." Beth repeated the word. That had to be the name of the house. At least some things were clear now but that still left a lot of other things unexplained. She thought of the two children again and set off for home. She didn't want to be out here on her own, not if they were about.

Beth tried to think straight. Was it possible they really were ghosts? If so, why were they haunting her? Why were they frightening her? It was all so weird that she couldn't get her head around it. A few steps later she found herself on the doorstep, opening the door. Her head was aching and she didn't have any answers. She had to get some rest.

# Chapter 12

Soon after Beth went inside, Dad arrived home in his usual end-of-week high spirits. Worn out by the heat and dazed by the day's events, Beth was happy to sit back and be amused by his impressions of his new work colleagues until, much to everyone's surprise, she volunteered to go to bed early.

Once she was on her own she could try and think clearly. But it turned out to be more difficult than she had imagined. Her room was uncomfortably hot even with the windows open and she felt terribly tired. After long minutes of fruitless thinking, she lay down on her bed and closed her eyes.

Almost instantly she fell asleep but it was a light, fitful sleep, and she tossed and turned while images flashed through her mind. She was looking down Ferry Road towards the island. A large house was standing there, the name "Riverside" visible on one of the tall gateposts at the front. Then she and Jack were suddenly on the island playing. Only it wasn't her and Jack, it was the other children. They were playing in a large garden, at the end of which was a beautiful glasshouse.

The pictures faded away, only to be replaced by sharper, painful images. Beth saw herself coming downstairs but they weren't their stairs – they were old, dark stairs. At the bottom was the boy who wasn't Jack holding a torch ... she was arguing with him ... she pushed him into another room ... they were arguing, they fell down and a heavy black curtain ripped ... the boy ran away...

A black, empty silence fell over Beth. After what could have been hours, it was broken by a faint light and a voice coming from the radio ... Beth found herself standing by the window … then she was outside, it was raining … she could hear a buzzing sound, getting louder … a huge black shadow, like a giant insect was flying overhead, filling her vision … she was running, shouting … fear gripped her entire body as she heard a splash, a splash, a thud and then a boom followed by that terrible flash of light…

"Beth, Beth wake up. You're having a nightmare. Wake up. It's only a bad dream."

A hand was shaking her shoulder. Beth blinked through the salty water spilling from her eyes and saw her dad. The curtains were wide open and bright sunlight was shining into the room.

"Come on, come on. It's all over now."

Beth's ears picked up a buzzing sound. She shrieked, flapping her hands at a large black shape flying around the room.

"Hey! Hey! It's only a fly. Don't worry, I'll let it out."

"Wha … what's going on?"

"You were just having a dream but it's OK now." Dad's voice soothed Beth's nerves. "We let you lie in because you seemed so tired. It's just gone eleven now."

Beth glanced across to the clock in amazement.

"There's no need to worry. Just get your breath back for a minute. Now, are you OK? We've been a bit concerned about you the last few days. We've noticed that you're not getting on with Jack and you've been a bit preoccupied recently. You do like it here, don't you? Is anything wrong?"

Beth shook her head. What could she say?

"That's good then." Dad smiled. "Mum was worried you might be getting yourself worked up about silly things. Like that time you got me outside to deal with those burglars. Do you remember? I was about to clobber that badger with a cricket bat before I was stopped."

Not again, Beth thought, diving under the bedclothes. "It was a hedgehog actually," she shouted through the sheets.

By the time she resurfaced, Dad had left to get brunch. Beth hugged herself as she

124

remembered what she had dreamt – the old house on the island, the two children, the terrible fear.

Dad was right, it had been a bad dream – her second bad dream. Why was she getting them? The two children had been in it again. Who were they? Why was she seeing these things? Was there some point to them or was she going slowly mad?

Her thoughts were interrupted by the smell of burning food wafting upstairs, closely followed by Dad's shout of "brunch's up". She went downstairs. After pushing the charred lumps of food around her plate for a few minutes, Beth was no closer to any answers.

During the meal, Dad told her and Jack that Mum had gone off to the supermarket and was expecting them to keep out of trouble before Gran's visit. Beth tramped dejectedly upstairs. She sat on her bed, head in hands. There was no need for Dad to worry; she was so tired and so hot that she could hardly stay awake. She blew some air on to her forehead and looked out of the window. Nothing was moving. The river, the trees and the bushes were so still it was almost as if they were waiting for something to happen. On the distant horizon, dark clouds were stacking up on top of each other.

Beth didn't know how long she had been staring out of the window. She was started into action by a cool breeze blowing on her face. She blinked. Out of the corner of her eye something moved. Just visible under the radio was a piece of yellowing paper, fluttering in the breeze. Seconds later, Beth had gently lifted the radio and was holding what turned out to be a scrap of old newspaper.

"*Tragedy strikes at Riverside…*" The headline made Beth jump. She looked at it again. The rest of the page had been ripped off. All that was left on the back was half an advert and the date at the top, 25th August 1941. Beth went pale. "That's fifty years ago tomorrow."

What was the tragedy at Riverside? Where had the paper come from? Beth paced up and down frantically in an attempt to concentrate. The radio! That was it. When she had brought the radio home it had been wrapped up in an old newspaper. A scrap of it must have caught under the radio when she had torn the rest off.

So what had she done with the rest of the newspaper? Beth checked her bin only to find it was empty. It must have been emptied out. She sprang into life and ran downstairs. She jumped down the last two steps, almost knocking Jack over. He dropped the bag he was carrying and it landed ·with a metallic clunk.

"Oi, watch it! What's the rush?"

"I'm trying to find something important. Get out of the way."

"You can't talk to me like that. Mum and Dad have gone into town to pick up Gran from the station. They'll be gone for a couple of hours and they left me in charge."

"Big deal. Just let me go, Jack. This is important."

"Oh, yes? It's not something to do with your

crazy ghost chase, is it? Well, while you've been wrapped up with your stupid ideas I've been busy too."

Despite her rush, Beth stepped back and looked at her brother. His voice contained a note of barely concealed excitement. "OK, OK," said Beth. "What are you up to? What's in there?"

"Ah, ha. No peeking." Jack smiled. "Let's just say I'm going on an expedition."

"What?" For the first time Beth noticed that Jack was holding a torch in his left hand. Behind him in the lounge was a large bag. "This is no time to be cryptic. What have you got in here?"

Beth pushed her way past him towards the bag. Her brother grabbed her before she could open it. She struggled against him and they banged into the wall, clicking on the light switch. Beth fell over, taking Jack with her. They rolled around wrestling each other until... RRRIP. Beth and Jack stopped at the ominous sound. They looked up to see the damage. The lounge curtain had managed to get caught under their feet and had ripped all along its length.

"Now look what you've done," yelled Jack. "Mum and Dad will be furious."

"It wasn't my fault," Beth shouted back. "You shouldn't have got in the way with your silly games. Just grow up, will you?"

"That's funny coming from you. I'm not staying here – you can tell them what you've done. I'm going to my new den. I'll fix it up and I'll stay there. You'll be begging to come in but I won't let you."

"Fat chance!" Beth retorted, stepping over the hammer and shovel that had fallen out of the bag. "Do what you want. See if I care!" Ignoring the taunts that followed her outside, Beth strode out to the bins, slamming the back door behind her. She was so furious that she upturned the bins and began a frantic search for the newspaper. Eventually Beth found what she was looking for amongst the mouldy food remains.

She unstuck the sheets of paper and matched the torn-off scrap to the front page. Brushing off some congealed sauce, she devoured the main story. Below the torn line was a black and white photograph of a smoking ruin. Beth recognized it as the glasshouse. Standing nearby in awkward poses were three dishevelled people.

The caption below the photo jumped off the page. *"Warden Stevens, Mr White and Mr Barnes pictured at the scene of the tragedy."*

This was incredible! Beth looked closely at the faces in the photo. After a few seconds she could make out the similarities between the present-day baker and grocer and their fathers. Matching the Bill Barnes who she had seen yesterday with the young man in the picture was more difficult but at last she recognized him by the nose and the shape of his head.

Her eyes moved down from the picture to the text. *"Last night tragedy struck Riverside House, on the island at the end of Ferry Road..."* Beth's heart pounded. The tragedy had happened the day before the paper was published. That meant it had happened on the 24th of August, 1941 – exactly fifty years ago. She read on. "*...when a lone German bomber dropped its bomb load on the Barker family's residence*." So that was the name of the family who lived there. "*Caught in the blast was Jonathan, aged 9, who died instantly. His sister Elizabeth, aged 12, was also injured and is currently in hospital...*"

Beth gasped as if she had been punched. Now her mind was racing. Elizabeth and Jonathan were her and Jack's real names. Fifty years ago today, two children with the same names had been caught in a bomb blast by the glasshouse. Last night's dream flashed before her eyes. Coming down the stairs, the argument, the pushing, the ripped curtain. It had all happened. She and Jack had just re-enacted exactly what she had seen in her dream.

Suddenly everything made sense. Her dreams had been warnings, premonitions. As well as seeing what had happened fifty years ago, they were also showing her what would happen tonight. History was about to repeat itself! She hadn't imagined the two children after all. They were the ghosts of the children who had lived at Riverside House. They were not dangerous. They had not been trying to frighten her, they knew the danger she and Jack were in and had been trying to warn her away from the glasshouse. Beth flinched as she remembered the buzzing sound and the dark shadow she had seen before that terrible flash of bright light. Now she knew what it was – it had been the bomber flying over her head. The bright light had been the explosion!

Fear clutched at Beth's heart with icy fingers. Where had Jack said he was going? His den? It had to be the glasshouse. He was carrying a torch and tools to work there. Fifty years ago, Jonathan Barker had been killed by a bomb landing near the glasshouse. Now she had been warned that the same terrible event was going to recur unless she could stop it.

Beth stood frozen to the spot. Total silence seemed to cloak the island. Then, distant at first but becoming louder with every second came a sound that chilled the blood in Beth's veins – the angry buzz of an aircraft's engines.

# Chapter 13

Heart pounding, brain racing, Beth leapt into action. She darted around to the front of the house just in time to see Jack heading towards the trees sheltering the glasshouse.

"Jack, Jack!" she bellowed. Her desperate shout went unheard – she was too far away. Beth ran for her brother's life. She broke into a sweat as soon as she began sprinting. The hot, humid air seemed to suck the breath from her lungs and the energy from her legs. Urging herself to go quicker, she dashed across the island. The sound of the plane's engines was getting louder. She glanced up quickly but it was invisible among the thick, low clouds.

"Faster, faster." Lungs screaming and limbs aching, Beth forced herself on. Up ahead she saw Jack stop on the edge of the copse. He had heard the plane and was peering into the sky.

"Run away, get under cover." Inside Beth was screaming, although she was too breathless to shout out a warning. Each step was bringing her nearer; she just needed to get a little closer. Up above, the hum of the engines was turning into a buzz. Then Beth heard a clunk. The sound of the engines changed as they struggled with the extra wind resistance. Beth could picture the bomb doors opening. She knew what would happen in just a few seconds.

Summoning up all her remaining energy, Beth took an extra long stride then launched herself through the air. She seemed to hang there for seconds before hitting Jack and knocking him backwards towards the bushes. Beth lay on top of her brother who was staring at her, goggle-eyed with amazement.

"Close your eyes and cover your ears," she yelled above the scream of the plane. Muscles tensed, she waited for the explosion…

Thirty seconds later, nothing had happened. Beth was pressing her hands over her ears so hard that they were hurting. Gradually, she dared to relax. As she moved her hands away she could hear the plane receding. She closed her eyes – still there was no explosion. After a few moments she could feel Jack, who was forcing the breath back into his lungs, wriggle underneath her.

Beth glanced up in time to see the tail of a plane, wheels lowered, flying below the cloud level. It had flown over their house and was heading towards the airport. Beth gulped for breath, slowly moving off her brother.

"What…? What the … what are you playing at?" Jack panted out between huge gulps of air.

Beth pointed up to the distant plane. "It was … the ghost plane…"

"What ghost plane? What are you talking about? That was a British Airways 747. Have you gone completely totally barking blooming mad?"

"I … I don't know…" Her voice trailed off. She was feeling confused, dispirited and drained. What had she done wrong? Why hadn't it happened as she had thought? She sat on the ground, staring at the earth, trying to understand.

In the meantime Jack got grumpily to his feet. He picked up his torch and bag, then stared down at his sister, eyes flashing with temper. "I don't know what's got into you recently. I'm off now. I'm going to fix that glasshouse up so it's brilliant. All it needs is a bit of work to make it into the perfect hideout. And you won't be allowed within a mile of it – ever! So there."

With that Jack stomped into the copse, angrily swinging the torch at branches in his way. Long after he had disappeared, Beth stayed put, her gaze fixed on the ground. By her left foot she saw a worm slowly burrowing its way into the earth. Beth wished she could do the same. Questions pounded relentlessly at her, repeating themselves over and again. She glanced upwards. Black clouds darkened the sky and a breeze had begun to disturb the heavy, still air. She flicked at the black flies buzzing around her. Her nostrils twitched. The heady, rich smell of pollen whirled around on the wind, filling her head and swamping her brain.

Beth got up dejectedly and dragged herself back the way she had run a few minutes ago. How could she have been so stupid? How could she have made such a fool of herself? She stood indecisively outside the front door, hesitating, not wanting to go in. So she had been wrong to think there might be a ghost plane, but surely the children and the dreams had to mean something. The warnings of danger had seemed so clear. She couldn't believe that she had been wrong about it. There had to be something else. Had something happened fifty years ago that she had missed? The newspaper might not have told the full story.

It was madness. How could she find out what had happened that night? Beth was already on a knife edge. Her brain was working overtime. Nervous energy gave her sudden inspiration.

There was one way to find out what had happened, Beth realized. It had been staring her in the face when she had studied the photograph. She would ask the one person who had been there fifty years ago – she would ask Bill Barnes.

The breeze had got stronger and turned into a swirling wind. Beth walked into it as she turned her back on home and marched over the creaking bridge on to Ferry Road. She had just passed the first cottage when a lightning flash lit up the sky. Rain spotted the pavement, falling to thunderous accompaniment. The drops grew heavier and thicker. For the second time that day Beth started to run. She knew where to head for.

She arrived, shivering outside the boathouse. A cold wind was blowing, chilling Beth through her soaking hair and clothes. She knocked loudly then pushed the door open. Once inside she stood still, rubbing her arms and trying to stop her teeth from chattering.

"Hello, Mr Barnes? Are you in here?"

*Crack*. Outside, lightning forked into the ground. In the burst of white light Beth saw streams of water pouring in through holes in the roof, hitting wooden beams and showering to the ground. At the far end of the boathouse the river was suddenly lit up. Against the water's choppy surfaces, Beth spotted the silhouette of the rowing boat. A feeling of fear overtook her, intensifying her loneliness. What was she doing here? Behind her the door banged shut in the wind. The thought that she should leave flickered in her consciousness before she stamped it out.

"Calm down, calm down," Beth muttered to herself. Then she screamed.

"Wha...!" replied the person who had appeared in front of her. There was the sound of wood scratching on wood then a flame flickered into life and Beth saw the grizzled face of Bill Barnes.

"Oh. It's you, is it?" began the ferryman. "What are you doing now? Trying to frighten the life out of me again?"

"Oh no," Beth replied. "I was just—"

"Just snooping, eh? What are you doing here? How did you find this place?"

"I … I'm sorry. I … I sort of stumbled across this place yesterday and saw you here."

"Oh, so that was you, was it? Well, this is private property and I don't like trespassers. Go on, scram, and you can take your bread with you."

"Oh, so that's where I left it. I'm sorry. I didn't mean to startle you and I don't mean to trespass. Please, just listen to me for a minute."

"I've got no time to listen to you. Go on, get going. Leave me in peace."

"Mr Barnes. Just hear me out for a second. It's terribly important. I know what happened fifty years ago tonight. I know about the bomb. I know about the children who used to live in Riverside House."

Beth's words had an immediate effect on the ferryman, which was heightened by the flickering light. His thick eyebrows arched upwards while his eyes widened hugely. A

140

second later, pain spasmed across his face then the light went out. Beth heard muttered swearing, and she turned to run away only to feel a strong hand on her shoulder. Her attempts to struggle only succeeded in tightening the grip. She couldn't make out anything in the sudden blackness although her ears heard a clank of metal nearby.

"Don't struggle, you little pest," boomed Mr Barnes. "There, that's better."

A red glow spread through the boathouse and at the same time the hand was lifted from Beth's shoulder. The boatman took a few steps into the boathouse where the water was slapping against the wooden pier. He planted a lamp on a wooden crate, motioning Beth to sit beside it. The lamp threw a warm light over the interior of the boathouse. The rowing boat, glowing with care and attention, bobbed in the choppy river water.

"Come on, come on," the ferryman sighed. "I'm not going to bite your head off."

Beth nodded. She stepped over coiled ropes, taking care not to tip over an old paint pot, and sat down opposite the boatman. She regretted trying to run away from him, now he just looked like a lonely old man.

"I suppose it had to happen one day," he sighed. "When I saw you on the street then down at the old glasshouse I thought it might come to this. So what do you want? What do you know about that night fifty years ago?"

Beth thought for a few seconds before beginning. "It all started when we moved in. I felt there was something strange about the glasshouse. I had these dreams. I saw two children who looked like me and Jack and I saw the old house on the island. They were frightening dreams and I didn't understand them until I discovered what had happened. I know that a bomb fell fifty years ago and ... well, it sounds crazy, but I thought I was being warned about some sort of danger. I actually thought there would be a ghost bomber."

She paused but she could see that she was being listened to with great attention. "I was wrong but I just can't get rid of this feeling that I was being warned – that there is still danger out there. And then I thought of you. I know that you were there after the bomb fell…" Beth took a deep breath. "And I wondered if you knew something. You acted so strangely when you met me. Then I found out that you had sworn never to go out on the river but you had a boat and that you had argued with your friend…" Beth hesitated. "Why were you at the glasshouse when we saw you? Will you tell me? Is it all connected with that night?"

Bill Barnes stared at the floor for a few seconds, shoulders slumped. He screwed up his eyes, took a deep breath and began. "I knew it was only a matter of time. You look so much like the girl, it's brought all the memories back… This is very difficult for me… You have to remember that fifty years ago it was wartime. Things were going badly for me and for everyone. The races had been closed down and there were no picnickers. There was rationing, bombing – it was terrible!"

The ferryman paused to collect his thoughts

before continuing. "Practically my only customers were the family who lived in Riverside House. They had a little business on the road. Lovely people they were, especially the kids. They were lively and cheeky – and they loved my boat."

During the pause, Beth heard the sound of the storm raging outside, beating on the boat-house roof.

"But they couldn't give me enough fares to survive. I tried my hand at a few things but none of them worked out. I was getting desperate, I didn't know what to do. And that's where my old mate, Dave, came in. He is – he was – the greengrocer then. His boy has taken over now. Anyway, Dave and me were best mates. You know, we went to school together and grew up on Ferry Road. Dave was always a bit of a wheeler and dealer even when he was young and he was the same when he grew up. You see, it was the war and things were scarce. There was rationing. You wouldn't believe how hard it was to get hold of things you take for granted now. Things like bananas or grapes, you just couldn't find them… So that was Dave's big idea."

"What was? I don't understand."

"I haven't told this to anyone for fifty years so it can wait a few seconds longer… You comfortable? Good. Well, he knew Riverside House and the garden well and he knew that the glasshouse wasn't being used. The children's dad had been called up into the army and in those days you just didn't grow tropical plants or things like that. So, that was when Dave had his brainwave. He could get all sorts of fruits but he needed somewhere to hide them. His plan was to store them in the glasshouse. They would be safe there, it was on an island and no one would search it. Once they were ripe he would sell them at a good price."

Beth's eyes opened wide. Surely this wasn't all about bananas?

"I know it seems stupid now but it didn't then," the ferryman continued. "Anyway, I didn't know that was the plan until after that night. All Dave had told me was that on certain nights, I was to let him 'hire' my boat and no questions asked. I was desperate so I agreed. And that was what happened. I got paid once a week and I kept my mouth shut. Everything worked a treat until that night fifty years ago."

"So what happened? What went wrong?"

"Dave was getting more and more worried about what he was doing. Looking back, I think he was feeling guilty. He decided to move all the stuff. He told me what he'd been doing and he asked me to help him – just that once. Like a fool, I agreed. So, we rowed out to the island and began moving the stuff."

"And you were seen?"

"That's right. Jonathan must have spotted us and come running down the garden. We had pushed off and were rowing back to shore when we saw the bomber. When the bomb exploded it caught the lad and his sister by the glasshouse."

"And that's why you fell out with Dave?"

"Yes," sighed Bill Barnes. He was holding his head in his hands. "We didn't know anyone had been killed until later. Dave told me to row back to his shop and hide the stuff."

"But why?"

"Because what we were doing was illegal. I wanted to tell people but Dave told me to keep quiet."

"And that's why you argued?"

"Yes, and that's why I swore never to go on the river again. If I hadn't rented my boat out to Dave or gone out that night then those kids wouldn't have been caught by the bomb. And I've kept my word ever since."

"And did you ever make it up with Mr White?"

"No. A few days later we were both called up into the army. Dave was killed and I was wounded. It seemed like due punishment for what we did. A few years after the war I came back to Ferry Road, I didn't know where else to go. Obviously things had changed. The family had gone, their business had closed down and Riverside House had been demolished. I tried to forget what I had done and I hadn't been back to the glasshouse until I saw you. That brought all the memories back and I walked across the bridge to that terrible place…"

Beth looked into the ferryman's bloodshot eyes and felt her own fill with tears. "There's one thing I don't understand," she muttered. "Why did the plane drop its bombs just there?"

"Well, that is a good question." Bill Barnes rubbed his hand across his chin. "I remember now. We thought we had been spotted when we saw a light appearing in the house. That's why we ran straight for the boat and pushed off. It was unusual to see a light because there was a blackout. All street lights were turned off and we were supposed to hang these heavy curtains at the windows to stop any lights showing through."

Beth's eyes narrowed. In the first dream, she had seen light spilling from a window and in the second she had seen what had happened. The curtain had been ripped in an argument between the two children. It was the light from that window that had guided the bomber. If only they hadn't argued… Beth tried to imagine how the girl must have felt when she had heard the bomber, knowing that her brother was in the garden. She could see her rushing outside only to be hit by the force of the explosion that killed her brother.

Bill Barnes interrupted her reverie by standing up. "This is a terrible night," he muttered hoarsely. "It's just like the night that has haunted me for fifty years. I can still see that plane, like a great black shadow flying overhead."

Beth nodded. Her mind flashed back to that first dream when she too had seen the bomber flying over. It was suddenly so real, each detail so vivid. The sounds of the plane's engines filled her ears as it dropped its deadly load of bombs ... of bombs. A shudder ran through Beth's body. "I've got it," she yelled. "That's what this business has been all about. It *is* a warning. I can remember it now. In my first dream I saw the plane drop four bombs. I heard a splash, a splash, a thud and then boom. The splashes must have been two of the bombs hitting the water and the boom was the one that exploded."

"So what does that mean?"

Beth looked directly at the ferryman. "It means that the third bomb must have hit the island but didn't go off. It means that Jack is out on the island with an unexploded bomb!"

# Chapter 14

"**C**ome on," Beth yelled. "We've got to reach him."

Bill Barnes needed no prompting. Grabbing the lamp by its handle, he led the way out of the boathouse. Beth, just one step behind, struggled to keep her footing as rain lashed down on her and the wind whipped around her, tugging at her clothes and pulling at her hair. The lamp swung wildly in the gusts while a roaring sound filled their ears.

"Be careful. It's a wild night. Just look at the river." Bill held out the lamp while yelling above the din. Beth followed the swinging arc of light as it illuminated the path, puddles lining the river bank and the river. She caught her breath. The storm had transformed the river; its waters had become fast-flowing, flecked with angry white waves and strong swirling currents.

"The river's flooding," yelled the boatman. "The storm's hit us at the same time as high tide. The river banks are under water."

As the light reflected off the water at her feet, Beth realized that what she thought were puddles actually marked the level of the river. They splashed on along the towpath. After a few seconds, she saw that Bill Barnes was beckoning her closer.

"This'll be a test for your new roof," he roared. "Keep an eye on that light. Aha. There's the road; now we can just follow it to the bridge and…"

His final words were drowned out by the rush of the river but Beth could see from his face that something was wrong. He was pointing ahead and holding the lamp up high. It took a few seconds for her to work out what he had noticed. All she could see was a stretch of river between the bank and the island. It was only when the lamp swung to and fro, casting its light on the shore, that she spotted the end of the road. The tarmac was jagged and crumpled as if someone had torn it away.

"The bridge – it's gone! It's been washed away. It was only temporary, it wasn't built to stand this sudden flood."

Beth stared across to the island. Maybe in this weather Jack would have abandoned his crazy idea and gone inside. Her eyes strained to focus through the driving rain. She could see a bright light. It was coming from the window with the ripped curtain. From there she could work out where the glasshouse was. To the right she spotted another, fainter beam of light – a torch. Jack must still be out there working.

There was no time to lose. They had to get on to the island, but with the bridge gone Beth realized that there was only one way. She looked at Bill. From the expression on his face, she could tell that he had been think-ing the same thing.

"I can't do it! I swore I'd never go on the river again." The boatman's voice was shaking.

"But you've got to. Please, it's the only way. No one else could do it but you. You've got the boat and the know-how, please!"

The boatman didn't move. "I'm too old and I haven't been on the river for fifty years. It's too dangerous – we'll all get killed. It's better if we call the police. Or wait for your parents to get back."

"No, no. It will take too long. Mum and Dad have gone to pick up Gran in town – they're bound to be delayed by this weather. The police will be far too busy as well. And anyway, what will we tell them? They'll never believe a story about an unexploded bomb. Come on, back to the boathouse. It's our only chance."

Beth could see the pain etched on Bill's face. He stood still, wrestling with his feelings.

"I can't afford to waste time like this," Beth said, snatching the light from him. "What happened fifty years ago happened. You can't change the past but you might change the future. I'm going to try at least. Are you coming, or not?"

Still the boatman did not move. Beth threw him a sharp glance then she turned around and headed back to the boathouse. By now the river had risen even higher over the towpath. She found herself wading through water that was up to her knees. She kept her eyes on the boathouse while listening out for the sound of someone behind her. She heard nothing – Bill was not coming. Beth pushed the disappointment to one side while she concentrated on the task ahead.

Soon she was kneeling beside the rowing boat. It was bobbing in the choppy water, the waves banging its gleaming hull against the pier, leaving traces of paint on the wooden planks.

A pair of oars was lying across the seats. Beth gingerly stepped aboard and once the boat had stopped rocking, she crawled towards the stern. "Come on, come on." She struggled to unfasten the mooring rope. Bill had done a good job tying up the boat. The coarse, rough rope chafed her hands, yanking at her nails. "Oww! Stupid knots." Still they wouldn't move. Beth sucked in her breath. She had to stop for a few moments; her palms were red raw.

She turned her attention back to the knots. After a few more fumbling attempts, her hands were on the verge of bleeding. She couldn't give up although she could hardly bear to grip the rope. Beth felt a wave of sickness wash through her. A bitter taste rose in her throat. She couldn't let herself be beaten now.

SWISH. Suddenly the rope went slack. Beth fell backwards into the boat, banging her head on the sharp blade of an oar.

Rain falling on her face brought her round. She shook her head, then wished she hadn't. Her head was throbbing and a lump was forming where she had hit it. She was lying in the bottom of the boat which was rocking violently from side to side. Beth cautiously manoeuvred herself upright just in time to catch a wave breaking over the bow. When she had blinked the water away she realized her predicament. She was alone in mid-river. She turned, swivelled around to grab the oars then stopped. Easily identifiable by his wide shoulders and confident, smooth style, Bill Barnes was rowing the boat.

"You're here. Thank you…" Beth let out a huge sigh of relief.

"And you're all right? You're not feeling too bad, are you?" came the booming answer. "What you said back there got me thinking. I knew you were right. I knocked on the baker's door and told him to get help, then I went back to the boathouse. I saw you bang your head and I managed to jump aboard as the boat drifted out into the river. If you're OK I need your help now. I want you to be the lookout – this current's awfully strong and it's bringing down all sorts of stuff. It's dangerous." To prove his point, a large branch clunked into the boat, making it veer off course.

Beth scrambled into position in the bows of

the boat. "Of course," she cried. "Head left — no, your left. That's it. Now pull."

The boat shot forwards, straining against the tide. It was barely a hundred metres to the island but they were against the current. Every time Bill strained at the oars they shot forwards only to be carried almost the same distance back between strokes. Beth could see her companion's shoulders flex then stretch with each effort. She willed him on, all the while keeping him on course.

The island loomed closer and closer. Gradually a gap appeared in the clouds, allowing light to filter through. From her position in the bows, Beth made out trees and bushes lining the shore. Rising above them she spotted the twisted ironwork of the glass-house. They were nearly there but the current seemed to be getting stronger. The boat was being battered by the water, dragged and swirled around. All Bill's efforts were only just enough to keep them moving forwards. Beth could tell that the ferryman was tiring. "One more stroke," she yelled. "I can almost touch land."

A breathless grunt greeted her news. With one last determined effort, Bill bent forward then pulled back. The bow of the boat seemed to leap over the water and land with a splash of relief in calmer water beside the banks of the island. While they drifted shorewards, the ferryman collapsed over his oars, fighting for breath. Beth knew that his energy was spent.

"Are you OK?" she asked.

Bill nodded, unable to speak.

"You'd better stay here and recover. And thanks again."

With that, Beth leapt ashore. The rain had churned up the river bank, turning it into a muddy morass. Still dizzy from the bang to her head, she slipped, struggled to her feet and ran towards the glasshouse. Branches whipped at her face while mud clung to her ankles, sapping her strength with every step.

"Jack! Jack!" she called. She was so out of breath that her cry was barely audible to herself. The trees parted in front of her and then she saw her brother. He had hung a ground sheet over part of the glasshouse to give him some shelter and had tied the torch to an iron bar. He was busy hammering away at one of the glasshouse supports, trying to bend it into a horizontal position.

He was OK, but Beth had to reach him. She felt danger all around. The bomb was somewhere nearby. After all these years, it would be unstable. Anything might set it off. Where was it?

A bolt of lightning lit up the sky. In that fraction of a second, through the driving rain, Beth saw two figures a few metres away from the glasshouse. A chill ran through her body as she recognized the ghostly children. Their eyes met Beth's. Their expression had changed; it was no longer so sad. At that moment the lightning died. The children melted away, but where they had been standing Beth saw a solid object, lying in the ground and giving off a dull grey glint. Rain drops exploded off it, showering in an arc. As she stared closer Beth made out a metal tail with grooved ridges – it was the bomb!

Beth forced air into her lungs and shouted. *"Jack! Look out!"*

Jack's hammer was in mid-swing when he heard Beth's yell and swung his head around. He was too surprised to stop the blow, and the hammer caught the iron support with a glancing blow. A brittle clang carried through the air. The pole shook for a few moments. It cracked. Beth took a step forward as the heavy girder began to fall through the air – heading straight for the exposed bomb. Arm outstretched, Beth skidded along the slippery ground.

"Owww!" The pole crashed down on to her forearm. For one long second it rested there before rolling away to squelch safely into the mud.

Beth lay flat out on the ground, tears of pain and happiness mingling with the rain and mud that splashed on to her face. She took a deep breath. She knew they still couldn't relax – not until they were safely out of range of the bomb. Jack was standing, hammer in hand beside the snapped iron support. He was so shocked at what had happened that he seemed unable to move.

Beth tried to lever herself up, only for a searing, white-hot pain to shoot through her arm. It hurt so much it made her feel sick. She collapsed to her knees. Her limbs felt as though they were made of lead. Beth watched her hands shaking uncontrollably. She suddenly felt terribly tired. Slowly, very slowly, she got to her feet.

"Come on, Jack. Snap out of it. Give me a hand."

At last her words got a reaction. Jack began to move, although only very slowly, as if he were sleep-walking. She led him away from the bomb and they stumbled towards the shore. Every movement jarred Beth's arm. She gritted her teeth and struggled on. Her vision seemed to swim and she lost her footing. A dark cloud of exhaustion and pain threatened to swamp her. She forced herself to get up. She carried on for another pace then she felt herself swaying, about to fall.

Before she hit the ground she felt a pair of

strong arms catch her. She looked up into Bill Barnes's face, then blacked out. She came to a few minutes later and managed to keep herself conscious long enough to see Jack beside her in the boat, then she slept.

# Chapter 15

Beth woke up after a long deep sleep. When she opened her eyes she saw that she was lying in her room. Sunlight was filtering in through the closed curtains. What time was it? What day was it, for that matter?

She turned over to reach for the clock. The stab of pain and the bandage on her forearm were sharp reminders of what had happened before. She could remember her and Jack being rowed away from the island but the rest was unclear. Images flashed up into her head: being carried on to dry land ... a crowd of people and police ... flashing lights ... the look of concern on her parents' face … Jack smiling … more faces … people closing in around her…

Beth slowly got out of bed and changed into some clean clothes. She tottered down the stairs, clearing her throat. It was dry and tasted horrible, as if she hadn't spoken for days. "Hello, is anyone there?"

Muffled shouts and running footsteps answered her question. Mum, Dad, Gran and Jack all appeared in the hall.

"You're awake, thank goodness!"

"How do you feel?"

"Just take it easy, Beth. Are you sure you're well enough to be up? Let me give you a hand."

She let herself be led into the kitchen and sat down at the table. All the questions were beginning to make her head ache. She took a slurp of the cold drink that had miraculously appeared in front of her. The coolness helped her throat. She held up her hand to silence the buzz. "Hey, I'm fine. I'm a bit stiff and a bit fuzzy but I'm fine. What I want to know is what happened. What did I miss? Where's the bomb?"

"The bomb's been made safe," Mum smiled.

"Yeah, these bomb disposal men appeared. They worked throughout the night. We stayed at the baker's and weren't allowed back on to the island until it had gone. It was a great big rusty thing. You should have seen it … oh."

Jack stopped when he realized what he had said. Beth smiled at him. He carried on quickly. "They said it was really unstable. It could have gone off at any time. Thanks for, well, you know, thanks for everything."

"That's OK. We were lucky. What about Bill, is he…?"

"Yes, he's fine," Dad replied. "You can see him later, but you need to rest first. It's either back to bed or on to the sofa and no arguing. I might let you talk to Gran in a while. Until then you mustn't get worked up or excited about anything."

Beth allowed herself to be taken into the

lounge and arranged on the sofa. She was plied with books and offers of drinks, then she was left alone. She found herself dozing off every few minutes. She could hear voices whispering outside and the sounds of her family trying very hard to be quiet. She thought about last night and about the two children who hadn't been as lucky as her and Jack. She wondered if they would still be by the glasshouse.

Beth was dragged back to the present by a quiet knocking on the door. "Hello, my dear. I've brought you some soup. Are you well enough for some?"

"Definitely. It's lovely to see you, Gran."

"Thank you. It's wonderful to see you too, although it wasn't so wonderful last night. You gave us quite a shock. I don't know, you've only been here a short time and look what's happened."

Beth smiled in reply. She could tell from the look on Gran's face that she was only teasing. "I know, I know. This is delicious soup. How was your journey?"

Beth listened, slowly sipping her soup, while Gran sat down beside her and told her about her adventures getting to their house last night. Her train had been delayed by the storm for hours. Eventually she had been picked up and driven home by Mum and Dad, but when they turned into Ferry Road, they had been surrounded by crowds of people and the police.

"It was quite an extraordinary evening," Gran continued. "The thing that occurred to me, though, is how did you know about that bomb?"

Beth choked on her soup. What should she say? Luckily Gran didn't repeat the question and instead she began talking about something else. "You certainly livened the place up. There are even some reporters about. I think the Ferry Road Fête should be a great success."

The fête had gone clean out of Beth's head. She quickly finished the soup. "Can I go?" she asked eagerly. "I'm feeling much better now I've eaten."

"Of course," Gran replied. "The others are already there. I promised I'd wait behind and escort you. I know you're not supposed to have any more excitement but we've got one little surprise in store."

Beth looked across expectantly, but Gran kept quiet as they left the house. Instead of heading round to the front, Beth was firmly but gently guided around to the back of the house. They walked across the garden towards the glasshouse. Beth could not suppress a shiver as she thought of last night.

The duo walked on in silence. The bushes and trees in the copse had been trampled down. Through the gaps Beth could see the ruined glasshouse. In front of it was a large crater where the bomb had been. A makeshift crane was still in position over the empty hole. An absolute silence hung over the place. Had the ghosts gone? They had tried to warn her and then they had helped her find the bomb. Surely now they would be able to rest?

Bushes moved and a twig cracked. Beth whirled around and glimpsed a boy wearing black shorts. She held her breath as the figure stepped into the sunlight.

"Jack!" Beth gasped. "What are you doing around here?"

"We've got something rigged up for you."

"Over there, dear."

Beth looked out at the river. Gradually a smile broke out on her face as she saw the sharp bows of a boat cutting smoothly through the calm water. In the centre of the boat, manning the oars, was a familiar figure – Bill Barnes.

"It was his idea," Gran whispered. "He said we should bring you here."

"That's OK," Beth whispered. "It's a good idea."

"Come on in," smiled the ferryman. "If you want to go to the fête."

Beth looked puzzled.

"Remember the bridge was washed away? This is the only way to and from the island."

They all got into the boat and Jack pushed them off. "Thank you for last night," Beth said. "It wouldn't have turned out right without you."

Bill shrugged in mid-stroke. The boat pulled away from the shore and Beth saw the Ferry Road Fête. It was bristling with life. Crowds of people filled the street, pouring into the stalls that had been set up. She saw the grocer and the baker rushing around, serving customers. Bill rowed the boat gently ashore and tied it up alongside the remains of the bridge.

Jack helped Gran on to dry land and they walked on along the street, leaving Beth and the boatman alone.

"I'm pleased to see you back on the river."

"I think it'll only be for a short time – until they rebuild the bridge."

"No!" Beth said, thinking of the empty glasshouse. "You've done enough now, you've cleared the debt. I was thinking about what you told me last night and I don't think you should be so hard on yourself – it wasn't your fault. You said that a light had suddenly started shining from the house. I think that a curtain got torn by Jonathan and Elizabeth during an argument – that was how the light appeared and guided the bomber to its target.

I don't know what they were arguing about but I do know that you must stop blaming yourself for their deaths."

"Do you really think I should?" asked Bill. Beth nodded and the ferryman smiled. "Do you think they'd forgive me?" he added quietly.

"Yes," Beth replied without hesitation.

Bill put his hand on her shoulder and squeezed. "Thank you," he said. "I'd like to think you're right." He paused to watch his reflection in the water. "I don't think I'm ready for all those people at the fête. I'm going to row back to the boathouse. Do you want to come?"

"Tomorrow," answered Beth. "I'll be OK here if I take things slowly."

She stepped ashore and waved at Bill as he began to row out into the river. Then she began strolling towards the crowds and her family. She thought back to what had happened the previous night and all the strange events leading up to it. She and Jack had been so lucky.

Beth stopped to avoid two men who were carrying furniture into a cottage. She was about to walk on when she looked more closely. The furniture wasn't going into a cottage, it was going into the old junk shop — only the shop was barely recognizable as its former self. It was in the process of being transformed. The objects she had seen through the window had all gone. The door and the windows had been cleaned and were being repainted.

"Excuse me, do you know what's going on?" she asked a man who was cutting down the plant that had covered the front of the shop.

"There are new people moving in on Monday; we're getting it all ready for them."

"But what happened to the lady who owned it? I was only in there last week. I talked to her. There were people in the back... What's wrong?"

Beth was aware that the man was looking strangely at her. "I think you must have been mistaken. You can't have seen a lady or anybody else in here. This shop closed down decades ago. It's been empty for years."

Surely the man was wrong. She had been given the radio here – the radio that had started her very first dream. The lady had wrapped it up in old newspaper – the newspaper that had carried the story about the bomb!

Beth stared at the shop. At that moment, the man pulled the plant away from the wall, revealing a sign that had been hidden by the branches. Beth could just read the cracked, faded letters painted there: Barker Antiques. Family Business, established 1929.

The last piece of the whole mysterious episode fell into place. No one would believe this. In fact, no one would believe any of it. Beth smiled. She didn't care. Everything had worked out right. Now the ghosts could rest. "Thank you," Beth whispered. "Thank you."

And with that, she turned away and walked towards the fête.

# Hippo Fantasy

Lose yourself in a whole new world, a world where anything is possible – from wizards and dragons, to time travel and new civilizations . . . Gripping, thrilling, scary and funny by turns, these Hippo Fantasy titles will hold you captivated to the very last page.

### The Night of Wishes
Michael Ende (author of *The Neverending Story*)

### Malcolm and the Cloud-Stealer
Douglas Hill

### The Wednesday Wizard
Sherryl Jordan

### Ratspell
Paddy Mounter

### Rowan of Rin
Emily Rodda

### The Practical Princess
Jay Williams

*If you like animals, then you'll love
Hippo Animal Stories!*

Look out for:

### *Animal Rescue* by **Bette Paul**

Tessa finds life in the country *so* different from life in the town. Will she ever be accepted? But everything changes when she meets Nora and Ned who run the village animal sanctuary, and becomes involved in a struggle to save the badgers of Delves Wood from destruction . . .

### *Thunderfoot* by **Deborah van der Beek**

Mel Whitby has always loved horses, and when she comes across an enormous by neglected horse in a railway field, she desperately wants to take care of it. But little does she know that taking care of Thunderfoot will change her life forever . . .

### *A Foxcub Named Freedom*
### by **Brenda Jobling**

A vixen lies seriously injured in the undergrowth. Her young son comes to her for comfort and warmth. The cub wants to help his mother to safety, but it is impossible. The vixen, sensing danger, nudges him away, caring nothing for herself – only for his freedom . . .

# Goosebumps

## by R.L. Stine

*Reader beware, you're in for a scare!*

*These terrifying tales will send shivers up your spine . . .*

*Available now:*

*Look out for:*

*Our favourite Babysitters are detectives too! Don't miss the new series of Babysitters Club Mysteries:*

*Available now:*

### No 1: Stacey and the Missing Ring
When Stacey's accused of stealing a valuable ring from a new family she's been sitting for, she's devastated – Stacey is *not* a thief!

### No 2: Beware, Dawn!
Just *who* is the mysterious "Mr X" who's been sending threatening notes to Dawn and phoning her while she's babysitting, *alone*?

### No 3: Mallory and the Ghost Cat
Mallory thinks she's solved the mystery of the spooky cat cries coming from the Craine's attic. But Mallory can *still* hear crying. Will Mallory find the *real* ghost of a cat this time?

### No 4: Kristy and the Missing Child
When little Jake Kuhn goes missing, Kristy can't stop thinking about it. Kristy makes up her mind. She *must* find Jake Kuhn . . . wherever he is!

### No 5: Mary Anne and the Secret in the Attic
Mary Anne is curious about her mother, who died when she was just a baby. Whilst rooting around in her creepy old attic Mary Anne comes across a secret she never knew . . .

### No 6: The Mystery at Claudia's House
Just what is going on? Who has been ransacking Claudia's room and borrowing her make-up and clothes? Something strange is happening at Claudia's house and the Babysitters are determined to solve the mystery . . .

**No 7: Dawn and the Disappearing Dogs**
Dawn decides to try her hand at *pet*sitting for a change, and feels terrible when one of her charges just . . . disappears. But when other dogs in the neighbourhood go missing, the Babysitters know that someone is up to no good . . .

**No 8: Jessi and the Jewel Thieves**
Jessi is thrilled to be taking a trip to see Quint in New York, and thinks that nothing could be more exciting. But when they overhear a conversation between jewel thieves, she knows that the adventure has only just begun . . .

**No 9: Kristy and the Haunted Mansion**
Travelling home from a game, Kristy and her all-star baseball team are stranded when a huge storm blows up. The bridges collapse, and the only place they can stay looks – haunted . . .

**No 10: Stacey and the Mystery Money**
When Stacey gets caught with a fake banknote, the Babysitters are astounded. Can *counterfeiters* really have come to Stoneybrook? The Babysitters have to solve the mystery, clear Stacey's name *and* save their reputation . . .

*Look out for:*

**No 12: Dawn and the Surfer Ghost**
**No 13: Mary Anne and the Library Mystery**
**No 14: Stacey and the Mystery at the Mall**